MW01716324

CROSSING THE LINE

CAT JOHNSON

CROSSING THE LINE

Cover art by BEVERLY MAXWELL

ISBN Trade paperback: 978-1-60202-126-6

ISBN MS Reader (LIT): 978-1-60202-127-3

Other available formats (no ISBNs are assigned):

PDF, PRC & HTML

Linden Bay Romance, LLC

Palm Harbor, Florida 34684

www.lindenbayromance.com

First Linden Bay Romance publication: July 2008

Dedicated to my muses in camo and combat boots.

In particular my Marine friend, consultant and sometime co-writer, Gary. He, while suffering through the African heat, allowed this inquisitive author to question him incessantly and steal and spin the mundane details of life at Camp Lemonier in Djibouti into this fictional tale, the original idea for which was his to begin with. I lucked out when the fates introduced me to this closet writer in desert camouflage wrapping and his fellow Marines, especially Chilly, who unwittingly became fodder for my tales.

As with all of my military novels, any mistakes made or liberties taken with the facts within are purely my own… creative license, author's prerogative and all that.

Visit the Links page on my website at www.catjohnson.net to learn where you can support our deployed troops or go to my profile at www.myspace.com/authorcatjohnson.

Prologue

Carrie Anne's breath came in ragged but steady gasps. With the endorphins rapidly firing through her brain, she knew she couldn't go on forever, but she was far from reaching her limit just yet, which was good because Alan displayed no signs of stopping or even easing up on her. Just behind her right ear she heard him grunting, his huffing and puffing far more labored than hers.

Like one would test a fine automobile, or a prize-winning horse, Carrie loved the feeling of pushing her body to the limit. Her confidence soared higher...apparently too high.

The first indication that she was in trouble was when Alan pulled ahead, passing her on legs that outstretched hers by a good foot. The second sign was when her blood felt as if it had reached the boiling point but for some reason, the very tippity-top of her head felt ice cold. Medically speaking, that probably was not a good thing.

Bathed in sweat, Carrie pushed harder in spite of the strange warning signals her body sent to her to back off.

She was eighteen and invincible. The world was her oyster. She could have anything she set her mind to and had proven that time and time again. Young, healthy, in the best shape of her life, Carrie had been valedictorian at her high school graduation that very day, but it wasn't enough. She had to prove herself one more time. She had to do this or feel like a complete failure. She had to win this race against him or she knew she would regret it for the rest of her life.

If sheer force of will had been enough to put her over the top, she would not be staring at her best friend's back now. Why couldn't she pull ahead? It had to be that stupid side bet she'd thrown in at the last minute. If she had just left well enough alone, Alan would never have pulled enough superhuman speed from somewhere deep within him to beat her. He never had in the past. It had to be her fault he managed to now.

Worst of all the finish line loomed ahead of her, what she could see of it past Alan's large frame, and it was crawling with their mutual high school friends, some of them cheering for her, all of them shocked to see Alan in the lead.

She heard his triumphant laugh as his chest hit the makeshift finish line, a crepe paper streamer torn down from the party decorations and held on each end by Carrie and Alan's fellow track team members. Arms flailing to slow herself, Carrie came to an eventual stop just past the group.

Bending at the waist with one hand pressed to her side in an attempt to ease the pain there, she managed to glance up and see the congratulations Alan absorbed so happily.

The boys, predictably, slapped him hard on the back while whooping loud and victoriously. Through the haze of exhausted defeat, Carrie noticed Mary Lou break through the crowd and throw her shapely form against Alan's in a full body hug before she kissed him on one sweaty, reddened cheek. Carrie still had enough reasoning power left to think that this girl must really like him to be doing that before he at least toweled off.

Carrie knew she needed to cool down her body slowly, was very well aware she should at least walk a bit to work the lactic acid out of her muscles or accept the consequences later, but instead she dropped to the cool grass and lay there, eyes closed, unmoving except for the rise and fall of her chest caused by her still heavy breathing.

She felt them above her even before she opened her eyes and saw them, the ring of grinning boys staring down at her with a mixture of anticipation and triumph in their eyes.

Alan's face appeared among them. "You a'ight, Carrie Anne?"

Carrie managed a nod.

Alan's face broke out in a wide smile. "Good. I'd hate for you to die or something before you fulfilled your part of our little wager."

His posse of male supporters nodded enthusiastically while snickering and elbowing each other.

With a groan Carrie sat up, bracing her forearms on her rubbery legs for a few more minutes before she even could think about making an attempt to stand.

"I've never welched on a bet in my life, Alan James Innis, and you know it." She also never thought she'd lose this particular bet.

Alan nodded. "I know. That's why they're so excited." He hooked a thumb at his chortling cohorts.

This time Carrie's groan was more of a growl. As if losing weren't bad enough, now it had to be followed by complete and utter public humiliation in front of a group of her drooling male classmates.

Alan extended his hand to her and helped her stand. The

inevitable could be put off no longer. Once she was on her feet, he grinned. "I'll hold your clothes for you if you want."

"Yeah, thanks a lot," she grumbled, glancing around the group uncomfortably. "Could you all at least turn your backs while I get undressed?"

One boy frowned. "What the hell for? We're gonna see you nekkid soon enough."

Thanks for the reminder. Arms firmly folded, Carrie stood her ground. "I know, but the deal was I'd run through the party, not put on a striptease show for y'all."

"Come on, guys. Let's give her some privacy. The show will start soon enough!" Alan winked in her direction as he grabbed the shoulders of the two teens closest to him and spun them to face away from her. Grumbling the whole time, the others grudgingly followed suit.

Being naked in front of Alan was no big deal. They'd been friends with each other for as long as she could remember. He was the brother she never had. Even that beastly hot day they'd both stripped bare and jumped into the river on their way home from school had been strictly platonic, a matter of necessity, really. Neither had wanted to get their good school clothes wet, but the heat was too unbearable to not dive in and cool off. But there had been nothing strange about it. She didn't think of him that way, and he felt the same.

But this…this was totally different.

Procrastinating would not do her any good, so Carrie flung her tank top, shorts, bra and panties off as quickly as possible. Leaving her running shoes on, she took off at top speed.

The loud collective whoop from the group of boys heralded the exact moment they saw her streak past. Running at least as fast as she had during the race that had landed her in this predicament, she quickly covered the predetermined route, confining behind each of her hands her small but far too bouncy breasts the entire way.

When the awful deed was finally done, Alan, thankfully alone and without his male entourage, met her behind a bush with her clothes held in a bundle in one hand. He turned respectfully away as she dressed in the now cooled but still uncomfortably sweat-drenched things.

Once she was covered again, Carrie noticed Alan kicking at the ground with the toe of one sneaker, indicating to her he was feeling weird about something. When he finally spoke, she knew what. "Um, what you gonna do about that other part of our bet, Carrie Anne?"

That other part had never been in question. She'd known for years what she'd wanted to do, and first thing Monday morning, as soon as the recruiting office opened up for the day, she'd be there doing it. "You know what I'm going to do, Alan."

"I know what you said, but the side bet was if you won, we both went, if I won neither of us had to go." He glanced up at her hopefully.

She wasn't any happier about leaving her best friend for parts unknown than he was. Actually, the *parts unknown* didn't bother her in the least. Anywhere had to be better than the stiflingly small town in Mississippi where they had both been born and raised, but the leaving her best friend part, yeah, that hurt a bit. Maybe that was what inspired her to add the side bet last minute, the hope that Alan would change his mind and come with her. He hadn't and judging by the way he ran that night he had no desire to follow her into the Air Force and leave this shit town.

Carrie forced a smile and was about to reassure him they would still be best friends even after she left for basic training when Mary Lou sauntered up to Alan, a big red plastic cup held in one small, manicured hand.

With a quick, almost jealous glance at Carrie, Mary Lou tugged on Alan's arm. "You want a beer? I'll get you one."

Alan looked at Carrie before answering.

"Go on, Alan. I need to wash up a bit. I'll see you two later."

Carrie released Alan to the girl's possessive grasp,

sincerely wishing him good luck with Mary Lou because if he didn't get at least a good make-out session that night, Carrie knew she'd have to hear about it for days, and she wasn't in the mood. Being best friends with a boy often had its disadvantages, his slight obsession regarding girls being one of them.

Alan nodded, adding before he was pulled away, "Good race, Carrie. Really good."

But not quite good enough. "Thanks," she answered as he disappeared in the direction of the keg and into the darkness.

Chapter One

"Where the hell are you now?"

Tech Sergeant Carrie A. Armstrong laughed into the phone receiver at the disbelief in her long time friend Alan's voice.

"A base in Rota, Spain," she answered.

"Wow. Spain. Impressive. Did you get to eat some real, authentic Spanish food?"

"Nah, we had calzones in this little pizza place when we landed. One of the guys had been through here before last deployment and said this spot made the best calzones he'd ever had. It was pretty good." Although, after being on a military transport from the States for hours with nothing but bottled water and energy bars, cardboard would have tasted pretty good to her.

She heard Alan laugh. "Only you would eat calzones in Spain. But there's always tomorrow for you to get some local grub, I reckon."

"No can do. We're only here overnight." If you could call it overnight. Carrie had to meet the others at the rally point at o-three-hundred hours.

"And you're on your way to where in Africa again?"

"Djibouti."

"Damn! When you lost that bet of ours, I never ever thought I would be dooming you to exile in a place named Djibouti. I am sorry about that, Carrie Ann."

Carrie had trouble believing her destination herself, but not for the same reasons as Alan. When deployment orders had come for her, she figured it would be to Iraq or Afghanistan. Considering those alternatives, the Combined Joint Task Force's Camp Lemonier in the Horn of Africa didn't look too bad in comparison.

"You didn't doom me to anything. You know I was joining up anyway. The only difference was if *I'd* won that bet, *you* would be here with me." That would have been nice, actually. She missed her friend from home.

"I know. Why do you think I pulled that last burst of speed out of my ass and passed you right before the finish line? No offense, but I knew Air Force rules were probably not gonna be for me. And back then I didn't even consider having to live in Africa. What do you think you're gonna find there? My bet is heat, killer snakes, and mosquitoes the size of those bombers we used to go see at the air show. Not my idea of fun, Carrie, and I would be right there with you if you had won that race. Do you remember my kick ass finish to our run?"

She remembered. How could she forget? According to her watch, during their race she and Alan had averaged just under a six-minute mile for six long miles in the blood-boiling Mississippi June heat. Practically unheard of for a run that length, but the stakes were high. If Carrie won, both Alan and she would join the Air Force together. If Alan won, which he did, neither one of them had to join up *and* Carrie had to streak naked through their high school graduation party that night. Yeah, *that* wasn't too embarrassing.

Carrie had thought she and Alan were equally matched as athletes, even though he was half a head taller, and that they were equally determined to win.

She'd laughed at the bet, certain Alan would be the one running butt ass naked through the party. But Alan apparently had more incentive to win, and not his doubts about the Air Force, either. Carrie learned much later that his *incentive* that night was his new crush on Mary Lou

Hennessy, and it seems the feeling was mutual on the girl's part. Mary Lou was now Alan's wife.

Thankfully, Carrie had managed to get leave to attend her best friend's wedding, that trip being one of the far too few times she'd managed to get home since joining up.

Until Mary Lou, they'd both talked often about joining up together, from the time they were little. Carrie's uncle was a pilot in the Air Force during Vietnam. From the day he took them both to an air show and Carrie first laid eyes on those Air Force planes flying in formation she was hooked.

Twelve years later, Carrie was a Tech Sergeant and Satellite Communications Operator for the United States Air Force. And Alan? He was a proud father of two, happily married, but not so happily working in his father-in-law's hardware store back in their hometown in Mississippi.

Carrie couldn't help but wonder how things would have turned out for him had she won that race instead. His life would surely have been different. She knew for a fact Alan had never left the great state of Mississippi in his thirty years. He never even took classes at the community college, although he wrote to Carrie about that plan for a while right after high school while she was away in basic training. Carrie, on the other hand, had lost count of the number of places she'd seen as well as lived and she now had extensive technical training courtesy of the United States Military.

She also knew that if that race were run again today, she would beat Alan by a mile. She loved to run, so she did it often, which made the required Air Force physical training a breeze for her. Nowadays, Alan's idea of PT was bowling.

"What's in Africa, anyways? I thought the war is in Iraq," he asked, dragging her back from that night in June to the present.

Carrie shook her head. Maybe if Alan spent more time watching CNN and less time watching ball games on TV he would know. "Take a look at a map sometime. You'll see how important HOA is geographically in this war."

"HOA? You Air Force people and your codes for everything. I swear," he drawled in a southern accent that reminded her too much of home.

Carrie sighed out a small laugh. "HOA is the Horn of Africa."

"Oh. Okay, Miss Smarty Pants. Anyways, I'd rather have you safe in *HOA* cooling your heels on Uncle Sam's dime than shot down over Iraq. I'm happy you're going there."

She didn't bother to correct him. Bordering Somalia, a hot bed of discontent and a favorite place for terrorists to hide, and located within striking distance of the narrow waterway between HOA and Yemen where ninety percent of the world's oil passed through, deployment to Djibouti was not as safe or uneventful as Alan assumed. Though he was correct, it would be nothing compared to the hot zone in Iraq or even the Taliban-riddled mountains bordering Pakistan in Afghanistan.

"I worry about my good old friend, you know," Alan continued.

"Thanks, Alan." She worried about him, too, but for other reasons. Carrie kept that to herself and said instead, "Listen. This call is costing like six dollars a minute and my phone card is probably about to run out. But I will email you as soon as I get settled at camp."

"Sure thing, Carrie. You take care now, y' hear."

"You, too, Alan. A kiss to Mary Lou and the kids for me."

"Will do."

Even more homesick after that phone call, Carrie replaced the receiver in its cradle on the nightstand and looked around her small but private room for the night. She knew she would only get the illusion of privacy at Lemonier. She'd heard there were plans at the camp to install metal CLUs or container living units, which were basically private tin cans for the personnel to sleep in, but until that plan came to fruition, they would each be allotted a ten by ten foot cube cut out of a larger sleeping tent by canvas dividers.

Carrie should have been grateful for tonight's last bit of solitude, but instead she felt suddenly very alone. Stateside, and to be honest bored for the last few years, she'd thought she would welcome the change of being deployed. But this first night away she couldn't shake the homesickness, even if home had been base housing for a very long time now.

A knock on the door startled Carrie. Jumping to open it, she found one of the Airmen from her squadron standing there.

"Change of plans. Ten-hundred tomorrow at the rally point instead of o-three-hundred," he informed her.

Great, more time to sit alone in her empty room. She nodded once. "Ten-hundred hours. I'll see you then."

He returned the nod and was off to knock on the next door and pass the word, and Carrie was left to herself once again.

Unzipping the desert tan flight suit to expose her short-sleeved black t-shirt underneath, Carrie let the top half of the suit dangle around her waist as she wandered to the bathroom. She might as well brush her teeth, shower and get ready for bed. Maybe she could sleep through the homesickness. Once they landed in Djibouti and she was busy working, she'd shake this unsettled feeling soon enough, no problem…she just needed to get there already.

Marine Staff Sergeant Beau Adams ran full out until his lungs and thighs felt as if they were on fire. God, how he hated running. When the end of the run trail at Camp Lemonier came into view, he slowed to a jog, then to a walk, letting his muscles cool slowly and working out the lactic acid built up so he wouldn't cramp or get sore.

Before showering Beau wanted to check in and make sure nothing had come up while he was gone, so he headed toward his office. By the time he had crossed the camp, reached the maintenance office building and grabbed a bottle of water, his breathing was nearly back to normal.

Opening his office door, Beau found his buddy Crash inside.

Speaking of getting back to normal…

"Crash. When the hell you gonna be able to work out with me again? I hate running as it is. Doing it alone is twice as bad." Beau wiped his face with the hem of his sweat-drenched tank-top and waited for a response from his friend.

Crash glanced up from the new episode of *Desperate Housewives* he was watching on the satellite television in Beau's office. At least they had TV this deployment—a big

Ooh Rah! for Central Command and the Combined Joint Task Force for that little bit of home all the way in the Horn of Africa.

Crash shrugged noncommittally. "Usually when I get shin splints this bad, it takes a few weeks. Sorry. Not much I can do about it. How was the run? Besides the fact you missed me, that is." Crash grinned at him and didn't look all that sorry.

How was the run? It was fucking hot, as usual, but this being Africa that should be pretty obvious. In spite of that fact, he decided to mention it anyway. "Fucking hot." Beau downed half of the bottle of water and then added, "I saw three camels and a hyena."

Close encounters with the African wildlife, pretty much an everyday occurrence, were hardly worth mentioning, either. When their detachment first arrived in Djibouti nearly two months earlier, the first camel sighting had been a photo-worthy event. He'd learned that day to not mess with the camels. Mean sons a' bitches those animals were.

Good thing Beau ran regularly, even though he hated doing it. Running had built up his stamina, and he'd needed the speed that day when the damn pissed off camel had chased him. Crash had been no help, either. All he did was snap a picture of Beau running with the camel in hot pursuit while laughing so hard it was surprising he'd managed the picture at all.

Nowadays, Beau steered a wide berth of any beasts he saw. Usually, thankfully, the animals did the same.

Crash grunted a response to Beau's previous answer, half his attention on one of the TV housewives strutting around in her lingerie on the screen. Beau turned to go and leave him to it when Crash glanced up. "Oh yeah, Beau, I almost forgot. The OIC stopped by while you were out. There's a transport bringing in some FNGs. It arrives in an hour. You have to meet their plane when it lands."

Frowning, Beau figured he had best count himself lucky that Crash had been finally able to wrestle his attention away from the show during a commercial break and relay the order, since he would have been royally screwed with the officer in charge if he'd failed to show up to meet the FNGs.

Fucking new guys. Beau groaned. One of the unsung jobs of being a crew chief and a staff non-commissioned officer was playing welcome wagon for FNGs.

Great. Just what Beau wanted to do after a full twelve hour day of work and a long, hot run, stand out on the sweltering runway and meet some plane like frigging Tattoo on that old TV show *Fantasy Island.*

An hour and a half later, showered but no less cranky, Beau stood at the airfield waiting for the C-5 to park so the

FNGs could deplane from a flight that had arrived thirty minutes later than expected.

He took solace in the fact that at least he wasn't alone out there in his hostess duties. An Airman stood next to him, looking just as unhappy to be there. The rotator flight would bring in guys for his detachment as well as replacements from the rear back home for the other military branches in Djibouti. Troops from the Navy, Army, Air Force, and Marines, as well as some from Guam, all co-existed more or less peacefully there at the old French Foreign Legion camp that was now the Joint Forces' Camp Lemonier.

Beau considered how long it would take him to get the FNGs settled before he could get to the Cantina for a beer. Perhaps he could include the camp's well-visited nightspot on the welcome tour. There was an idea.

His appreciation of his own brilliance was interrupted by the Airman's comment as the FNGs began descending the plane stairs. "Hey, check out my new SatCom operator. Damn, she is hot! I'd heard rumors she was but I never believe talk like that until I see for myself."

Frowning, he glanced up with surprise. Beau supposed it was old fashioned, or chauvinistic, or maybe just plain stupid of him to assume the new SatCom operator would be male. Either way, he definitely would not have considered she'd be a hottie. But damn, the Airman was right. This girl was what Crash would no doubt refer to as a "Hocakes" the minute he laid eyes on her, meaning she looked good enough to eat and was totally doable.

Hoping he was mistaken in his assumption, but afraid he wasn't, Beau commented as casually as possible, "We're supposed to be taking a new SatCom operator up in one of our CH-53s for training tomorrow."

The Airman nodded, confirming his fears. "Yup, that would be her. You lucked out. Although, from what I hear, she's cold as ice. Don't get your hopes up about getting lucky with this one."

Beau raised a brow. Luck like that could be both good and bad. Females in the military spelled trouble in his opinion. He had been more than happy when his detachment to HOA consisted of only males. Keeping track of the men was enough work for him. That would be all he needed, to be worrying about the females under his command getting drunk and in trouble at the Cantina or worse, getting pregnant and in even more trouble.

Of course there existed a no fraternization rule on camp. No sex while deployed. That was the rule. Being caught violating this order, particularly a ranking officer, could end the careers of one or both parties involved. But in spite of that the PX there on camp still sold both condoms and pregnancy tests. Go figure.

It was obvious that when you put a bunch of lonely men and women in a foreign country away from their homes and families for long periods of time, making up rules specifying they not have sex for six months or more was just asking for trouble. Anyone who'd had to get up to take a piss about sunrise could be treated to the comic scene of quite a few males and females trying to sneak out of each other's tents unnoticed after a night of getting busy, proving that certain rules were made to be broken, even in the military.

Beau himself had been kept awake a few nights by noises coming through the canvas wall from the cube next to his. Female noises that his male neighbor Staff Sergeant Pearson could not possibly be making alone. Beau had always managed to keep his own dick happy by himself while deployed, both when he was married, and now that he was divorced. Fourteen years under his belt and only another six to retirement, he was not about to risk his career now. Not for a little pussy.

Beau sighed. His crew would no doubt be distracted by this hot Air Force chick, though, and it was his job to make sure they weren't. Thank god she had a reputation of being a cold fish. That might help him some. If only the rest of the women on camp were equally as cold and fishy. *Eeewww.*

That was an unfortunate choice of words on his part, making for quite the unpleasant image.

This whole female SatCom operator situation was more than he needed at this point in time. Except for an incident or two right after they'd arrived in HOA, Beau had been flying along real nice the last couple of weeks, giving him renewed hope that the rest of his deployment would be nice and boring and uneventful.

Yes, except for those couple of bumps in the road that he'd rather forget, things were good. But now, even at a hundred and twenty five degrees Fahrenheit most days, Beau imagined that after the arrival of this new chick it was going to get even hotter around there.

Oh well, at least Crash would be happy about the new addition to camp. The man enjoyed two things, nice scenery and a cold beer. With that thought, Beau remembered how much he really needed a brew at the Cantina, maybe more than one.

Chapter Two

"Damn! That new SatCom operator is some kinda hocakes. Huh?" Crash said a bit too loudly while nudging Beau in the ribs with his elbow as they exited the hanger after the following day's training.

Here we go, Beau thought. *Right on schedule*. Good old predictable Crash. Big and loud. That was how the man got his nickname to begin with.

Beau sighed and said noncommittally with a shrug, "I don't know. I guess so."

For better or worse, Air Force Tech Sergeant Carrie Armstrong was exactly what Crash so inelegantly said she was. Beau had managed to keep the crew on task during the training; his men were all too professional to do anything else while in the air. But now, after-hours when the work was done, that would be another story judging by the interested looks some of his guys had given her, before Beau gave them a look of his own, that is.

He couldn't fault the sergeant in any way for the attention being paid to her, though. She'd done her job and done it well, acting totally professional the entire time they were up in the helo.

The comments the Airman on the runway had made to Beau yesterday upon her arrival weren't totally accurate, however. Yes, she was good-looking, just like the Airmen said, but Beau wouldn't call her icy like that guy had. She was simply work-focused. But aside from that, she appeared friendly and pleasant enough to him.

Of course, Beau had treated her like the highly trained professional he knew her to be. She probably reserved the big chill for the guys who came on to her. He was sure he would see soon enough how she'd react to being hit on if the way Crash was already acting served as any indication of events to come.

Beau noted how Crash frowned at him now as he practically spat, "*You guess so?* She's the hottest thing to show up here since we arrived. What's up your butt today, anyway?"

The creases in Beau's forehead put Crash's frown to

shame. "What do you mean, what's up my butt? Just cause I'm not drooling over some tech sergeant and trying to get in her pants?"

They had been in the Marines together for years. Crash should know him better than that. Chasing skirts was not his style.

"You might be less ornery if you did try to get into somebody's pants. We'd all be a lot happier if you got laid, I think. And there's enough women 'round here. It doesn't have to be her. If she's not your type, there are plenty more where she came from. Just pick one."

Her being his type was definitely not the issue. The rules, however, were.

Yup, that no fraternization rule might as well have been written in sand on the hood of a humvee during a windstorm.

Crash continued, undeterred. "You're single again now. You can do more than just snap your own bean in your cube at night."

Beau groaned. Those canvas walls were way too thin, a fact he tried his best to ignore while involved in that particular act Crash had just referred to.

"My getting laid," *or not*, Beau added silently, "is *not* up for general discussion."

Crash rolled his eyes. "Yeah, whatever. You ready for

chow?"

He was more than ready, especially if it ended this topic of conversation. Beau nodded, feeling both relieved and hungry. "Good to go."

He thought that maybe if Crash had a mouthful of food, there would be less talk about Tech Sergeant Armstrong and Beau's sex life, and that would be fine with him. But his hopes for a change of topic proved short lived as, food trays in one hand and ice-cold Gatorades in the other, the two men came off the chow line and stood smack in front of the female in question who just happened to be sitting alone at one of the few tables with two available seats.

Beau stifled a groan at the wide grin that spread across Crash's face as he straddled an empty chair and plopped his tray down on Tech Sergeant Armstrong's table with a clatter of plastic.

Crash nodded to her as she glanced up.

Still standing, Beau asked, "Tech Sergeant. Um, are these seats taken?"

Beau figured the question was a bit late considering Crash's butt currently occupied one of the chairs and he'd already started shoveling food into his mouth with a distinctly smart-ass grin on his face. Still, he could always hope she'd say the seats were being held for someone so they could go sit somewhere else, far, far away at a nice safe distance.

She looked up at him with big warm eyes, the irises of which were hazel, almost green and flecked with gold. The edge of her black t-shirt peeked out from the neck of her flight suit. Beau imagined that her pert nipples, if he could see them, would be peeking through the thin fabric of the shirt thanks to the air conditioning in the Bob Hope Dining Hall cranking on high that day in an attempt to combat the sweltering African heat outside.

Beau quickly shelved that image and dragged his eyes back up to her face as fast as a naughty boy caught with his hand in the cookie jar, or more accurately in this case, the hocake jar.

Luckily, she didn't seem to notice as she shook her head and answered, "Nope. They're all yours. Take a seat."

Shooting a scowl in Crash's direction over her lowered head, Beau reluctantly sat and tried to focus solely on his tuna sandwich on whole wheat. He did a good job at it, too, remaining silent until the politeness his Georgia mama had instilled in him from birth got the better of him.

Barely even raising his eyes from his food, he said in her general direction, "Good job today, Tech Sergeant Armstrong."

She looked up in surprise at the compliment and then nodded curtly and said, "Thanks. It was a good training.

You've got a good crew working for you, Staff Sergeant."

Beau let out a short laugh. "Yeah. Most of them, most of the time, anyway." *When they weren't sticking their nose in his business.*

He noticed Crash grinning again and felt the urge to kick him good under the table. Combat boots could do some kind of damage if you aimed well enough. Maybe a nice purple bruise on top of his shin splints would remind Crash not to meddle in Beau's affairs, or lack of them.

Meanwhile, Beau was becoming more and more intrigued with placing the origin of her soft southern drawl. It was slight, but definitely there. It didn't sound like Georgia, or even the Carolinas. Maybe further west.

Wrestling his mind away from any more wondering, Beau went back to his chow, relieved the awkward but obligatory polite conversation part of the meal was over. His mama would be proud.

Between bites, Crash glanced up at him. "You running later?"

Beau nodded, happy they were talking about something normal and non-female related. "Yup. You coming?"

"Nope. My shin splints still hurt like hell. I don't want to push it too soon."

The conversation had the tech sergeant looking up with interest. "Where's the best place to run around here?"

Beau waited a beat, hoping Crash would answer. When he didn't, Beau said, "There's a run trail outside the gate. It's five miles total, out and back, measured and marked. Don't go running until nearer sundown, though. This heat will kill you if you try to work out in full sun."

She nodded, looking strangely excited at the thought of running in the heat, a feeling Beau could not understand or share. "Can you point out the trail to me after you're done eating?" she asked.

Before Beau could answer, Crash looked up at him and chimed in, "Why don't you two run together? You're always complaining you hate to run alone. Maybe you'll stay off my back for a while about being laid up if you've got someone else to push your sorry ass."

Now what could he say? No? "Um, sure, I guess." The urge to kick Crash grew stronger as Beau hoped the sergeant would say no to his offer.

No such luck. Instead, her eyes opened wide with excitement.

"Really? That'd be great! I haven't had a good run in three days. I could use one after sitting in a plane for two of them," she said.

Shit. He really didn't want to do this. Everyone on camp would think he was running with her to try and get into her pants. "I'm not going until seventeen-thirty," he said, hoping to dissuade her.

"That's good. I'll be ready. Where should I meet you?"

He held in a groan of frustration. "At the security gate, I guess. That's right by the start of the run trail."

She nodded and then stood, empty tray in hand. "Sounds good. I'll see you then." Smiling, she left.

The moment the woman was out of earshot, Beau turned on Crash. "What the hell did you do that for? Volunteering me to go running with her. Are you crazy?"

Crash grinned. "You need a run partner, that's all."

Beau shook his head. "You know what everybody's gonna think."

His supposed friend shrugged. "So what? What d'you care what people think?"

The truth was, Beau shouldn't care what people thought. And normally he wouldn't. So why did he care now? Maybe because this girl, with her pretty sun-lightened golden brunette hair that swung like silk around her shoulders when it wasn't confined in a bun for work, this stranger who only wanted to find a safe place to run after being cooped up in a plane for days, didn't deserve to have the camp assume she was already fucking around the day after she arrived. And it was all just because Crash wanted to get Beau a run partner so he wouldn't have to go himself. And more than likely, because Crash thought it would help

Beau get laid so he'd be in a better mood. Well, Crash's plan had backfired in a major way, because Beau's mood could not have gotten any worse than it was at this moment.

But besides his anger at Crash's interference, Beau had something else to consider. Why did the thought of people thinking the new SatCom operator was fucking around with him make Beau so angry and protective of a woman who was basically a total stranger? It had to be his southern gentleman values kicking in, that's all. You could take the boy out of the south but not the south out of the boy, he guessed.

Happy with that explanation, he went back to finishing his meal, hopefully in peace, until he caught the pleased look on Crash's face and literally growled at him.

"What?" Crash asked wide-eyed, acting all innocent.

Beau didn't bother explaining the obvious. Instead, he just shook his head, rose and dumped the few remaining bites of his sandwich in the trash, suddenly more annoyed than hungry.

Chapter Three

Carrie's lungs burned from exertion, not to mention from what had to be about one hundred degree Fahrenheit heat, as well. And this was supposedly the cooler portion of the day! But it felt good to run until her heart pounded and her limbs ached. She'd missed that feeling during the past few days of traveling and getting settled in camp.

Maybe it was the endorphins or dopamine or whatever else a body produced during good hard exercise that made her feel so good. Maybe it was simply that running was the one constant in her life of ever changing scenery. Carrie could run wherever she happened to be—home in Mississippi, an Air Force base somewhere in the US or even at a camp here in lovely Djibouti on the Horn of Africa.

And while she focused solely on her run, it didn't matter that the other female Airmen had not been exactly warm and fuzzy upon her arrival. It didn't matter that most of the men at camp spent more time staring at her boobs, what there was of them, rather than realizing she was damn good at her job. It didn't even matter that the one and only person who had been nice to her since her arrival looked less than thrilled to have her tagging along on his nightly run.

A quick sideways glimpse to check the progress of the Marine running next to her told her that Staff Sergeant Adams had gotten over his initial annoyance and, more importantly, that he was hurting now, too, just like she was. And like her, he wasn't about to be the first to slow down.

Why were all men so competitive? It was ridiculous. She should be the bigger man, so to speak, and slow down first so they both didn't end up collapsed on the run trail and food for the vultures she noticed flying lazily above them. So why was she still pouring on the speed in spite of the fact that every spare ounce of water in her body had already poured out in her sweat, drenching to near saturation her t-shirt and shorts?

Because years later, she was still as competitive as she'd been in high school, that's why.

Damn it. Heat exhaustion wouldn't do either of them

any good. Carrie bit the bullet and slowed down, just a tad, and Adams, who had been running even with her, immediately matched her new pace. Sneaking another peek at his face, she consoled herself with the knowledge that he looked grateful for the slower speed.

The crew chief had proven to be both a competent leader during her training in the CH-53E helicopter as well as an excellent running partner. No chatter or small talk. He didn't try to outrun her and prove himself the bigger man. Instead, he just kept up with whatever pace she set, no complaint, no discussion, no games, no crap.

He was her kind of work and running partner. Carrie hoped they could run together again. One thing she loved about running was that she could do it alone. But running with a partner, even in silence, did seem somehow easier than running solo, particularly in the heat when it would be all too easy to use the temperature as an excuse and give up for the night.

She glanced at him again out of the corner of her eye so he wouldn't notice and think she was staring at him. Besides being a decent runner, Beau Adams wasn't too bad to look at, either.

She took a moment to consider his assets. Barely a head taller than herself, he kept himself in good shape, obviously taking advantage of the gym there at Lemonier, judging by the muscles displayed openly by the armholes of his now sweat-soaked tank top. Light brown hair cropped in a short military cut framed good strong facial features punctuated by eyes that seemed to change from green to blue to a mixture of both, depending on the light—not that she had noticed, of course.

Carrie dragged her attention away from thoughts of Staff Sergeant Adams and that slow soothing southern drawl of his and had to concentrate on the fact that they were nearing the end of their run and had yet to cool down. She slowed the pace to an unhurried jog, then a fast walk. He adjusted quickly and matched her step for step, holding his side with one hand.

"You all right?" she asked.

He nodded, sounding as breathless as she felt. "Just a cramp."

She wondered exactly how long he'd been hiding that cramp in his refusal to show her any weakness. Typical stubborn man. The military was full of them.

"Walk it off," she huffed out breathlessly. In consideration of his pain, she lessened their progress to a slow walk now.

As Beau nodded his assent, Carrie glanced just past him and nearly tripped to a stop. Wide eyed she asked, "Is that a…"

He followed her gaze. "Camel? Yup. They're all over the place 'round here."

Okay. Since he didn't seem impressed or frightened by the camel sighting, she tried not to be also and went back to the earlier subject of their very brief conversation. "How's your cramp?"

"Better. I'll be fine but damn, I am dying for a cold bottle of water."

"You shouldn't drink water too cold after running in heat like this. I know you've been here at camp longer, but I grew up in Mississippi. I know about heat."

He grinned and hooked one thumb at his own chest. "Georgia. Born and raised. I'm familiar with heat myself."

Georgia. That explained the drawl. "Yeah, I guess you would know about high temperatures being from Georgia. I've been through *Hot-lanta* a few times myself."

He chuckled at her use of the well-known nickname for Atlanta and its reputation for extreme heat. The man had a great laugh and an even better smile. She smiled back.

"You still have family in Mississippi?" he asked casually while still breathing heavily.

Carrie nodded. "Yup, my folks still run the farm I grew up on along the Mississippi River. And my uncle's still there, too. He…my uncle…was a pilot in the Air Force in Vietnam."

"That why you joined up? Your uncle."

She nodded. "Yeah. When I was a kid I loved listening to him tell his friends stories about when he was an Airman. My mom was continuously buying me dolls, when meanwhile I kept asking for model planes. My parents weren't too happy about my decision to enlist, I can tell you that. But even graduating high school with honors, the career opportunities where I grew up were pretty limited. I wasn't going to stick around with hopes I'd make a career managing the local SuperMart after college. The only other alternative would be to get married right out of school and be barefoot and pregnant, raising a slew of kids in the bayou like so many of the rest of the girls I graduated with."

Which reminded her, she had to check out the internet situation on camp so she could email Alan and her relatives back in Mississippi. There was supposedly a coffee shop on camp that had internet hookups and she'd even heard a rumor of camp-wide wireless internet access that worked sporadically in the sleeping tents, but she had yet to investigate the truth of it. Good thing she had her laptop, in either case.

She'd inquire about that later but now, she was more curious about the man beside her. "What about you?"

Beau shook his head. "I joined because I didn't want to be barefoot and pregnant, either." A boyish smirk crossed his face, making her laugh.

Carrie rolled her eyes playfully. "I mean is your family still back in Georgia?" *And speaking of barefoot and pregnant, is there a Mrs. Adams and little Beaus running around?* she added silently.

"Mama and my sisters are still in Georgia. I'm stationed in North Carolina so I get back home as often as I can to visit. It's a five-hour drive on a good day with no weather or traffic. Not too bad."

Good to know, but that still didn't answer the wife question. "I was at Dyess Air Force Base in Texas when I was Stateside. Not as close to home as you, but I do have access to air travel when I need it."

He grinned again. "Yeah, being Air Force I guess you do."

She then realized with a strange mixture of relief and regret that they now stood in front of one of the many water stations set up on camp, but they were also in front of the maintenance tent where Beau worked. As much as she needed the water, she hated the conversation to end when it had barely begun, but they'd definitely reached the end of their run.

That was it then. Time to say goodbye and go shower.

"Good run. Thanks." She hesitated a beat before throwing out a last minute invitation hopefully. "Same time and place tomorrow?"

Carrie didn't realize she'd been anxiously waiting in anticipation of his answer until excitement flooded her when he nodded once and said, "Good to go."

Sweat poured down both sides of his face, leaving streaks in the dust they had both become covered in from the run trail, but all she could think about was how handsome he looked in spite of that.

While she was busy thinking about how she couldn't wait for their run the next day, he reached into the small shelter that served as a hydration station and grabbed them two plastic bottles, handing one to her. "Don't forget to drink lots of water, Tech Sergeant."

"I will. Thanks. And please, Staff Sergeant, while we're running, call me Carrie. It's too damn hot to be formal."

He laughed. "Yeah, it sure as hell is. But if I'm gonna call you Carrie, then you have to call me Beau."

She nodded, fingering the condensation dripping off the bottle he'd handed her and trying not to grin like a schoolgirl over the simple fact she could call him by his first name. "Okay, Beau. I'll see you tomorrow."

He nodded. "You surely will." Then he turned and went into the tent, leaving Carrie alone to wonder why, after all the men she'd met since joining up, this guy, after her only being here for two days, had captured so much of her attention.

Carrie didn't have an answer, but when she arrived back at her tent, she realized there was still a huge unexplainable smile on her face.

"Two beers, please." Beau slapped his and Crash's beer cards on the wooden surface of the Cantina's plywood-topped bar for the bartender on duty to mark off their first round of the camp's three-beer per person, per day, limit.

Although a big enough tip would sometimes lead to the guy on duty conveniently "forgetting" to mark off a beer or two over the course of the evening, even better were the nights that one of the guys on Beau's crew manned the bar. Beer cards didn't mean a thing then, and as long as no one got stupid drunk and made a scene, no harm, no foul.

Sliding the cash across the bar for the bartender, Beau noticed there were even more signatures added to the already graffiti-covered plywood bar top since the last time he'd been there. He and Crash would have to remember to grab a permanent marker from the office and commemorate their own time there before they left, but with months yet to go, he figured they had plenty of time for that.

After grabbing the two bottles from the bartender, Beau turned and handed Crash his beer and his card. It had been marked with a big black X. Seemed like tonight would not be one of those nights they could indulge in a few extra. Given that, Beau decided he better savor each one.

Crash glanced at the card with a scowl before putting it away in his wallet. He'd noticed the mark, too. "Thanks. Next round is on me."

Beau grinned good-naturedly. "You bet it is." Beers were ridiculously cheap there at Lemonier. No one would go broke buying a round or two, but they alternated anyway to keep things fair, each buying a round until their limit was reached.

Locating an empty table, Crash sat and then leaned forward and hissed, "So, spill. How was running with the hocakes? Did I hook you up or what?"

There was no frigging way Beau was going to admit to his meddling friend he had enjoyed his run with Carrie. But then again, he knew Crash thought she was hot, so why not rub it in a little bit that he had been alone with her getting hot and sweaty, even if it was only from running.

"You sure did hook me up. We both enjoyed it so much we're going again tomorrow."

The stricken look on Crash's face was worth a thousand words. "Really?"

Beau nodded. "Yeah. She's a damn good runner. Before we headed out she mentioned she's run a few half-marathons. We ran harder than I usually do with you, I can tell you that. You take your time recuperating from those shin splints. I'm fine running with her instead."

A frown crossed Crash's brow as he began playing with the sweat beading off his bottle. "So, all you did was run and then come right back? Right?"

This was too good! Payback could be a bitch. Crash liked to tease him about not hooking up at camp, about not showing any interest in any of the female troops while they were deployed, and actually, while they were Stateside, too. But it seemed that in spite of his teasing he never expected Beau to actually do something about it.

Crash's surprise at Beau's interest in Carrie was palatable. Beau decided to take advantage and tease him further.

"Hell no, we didn't just run. We talked a lot, too." He left exactly what they had discussed unspecified as further torture for Crash's meddling.

The creases deepened in his friend's forehead, and Beau had to suppress his urge to laugh. Particularly at the shocked look on Crash's face when Beau added, "I think I'm gonna request her for SatCom again next time we go up. Hell, probably for every time we go up. She's good at what she does."

Crash took a long swig but didn't say another word

about “Sergeant Hocakes”. Finally, peace and quiet. Beau took a sip from his own bottle to hide his satisfied grin.

Chapter Four

A tired Carrie made her way from the shower trailer toward the entrance of the female Airmen's quarters. Fresh and clean after another grueling yet invigorating sunset run with Beau in the African heat, she was looking forward to racking out now as much as she had begun to look forward to her daily runs with Beau over the past week.

She slipped past unnoticed, or at least un-greeted, by the chatty group of women seated in the white plastic chairs kept just outside the tent door and was heading for her sleeping cube when her neighbor popped her head out of her doorway.

"Hey, girl. Get yourself ready. We're leaving for the Cantina. Hurry up. I'll wait for you."

Surprised, it tock Carrie a few seconds to answer. "I don't know, Lawanda. I'm not much of a drinker and besides, I'm really beat."

Carrie felt totally taken aback. An actual invitation to join the girls? That was quite a surprise. Except for her neighbor, a tough inner city African American from Chicago, the other women in their quarters had treated Carrie as if she was beneath their notice. Even with Lawanda's friendly overature, Carrie still didn't think she wanted to spend the night with the others who never even gave her the time of day.

She guessed she couldn't blame the women at camp for being less than friendly since her arrival over a week ago. Cliques naturally formed among groups of women, even in the military, and she was the newcomer. The rest had all arrived together months ago. Carrie tended to keep to herself mostly, and had since she was a child, which is why she had very few real, true friends and people often assumed she was aloof. Truth was, she was shy, not stuck-up.

The other women's attitudes shouldn't matter much to her. She reminded herself again that she hadn't joined the Air Force to make friends. Carrie was there to gain skills, do her job, and hopefully make a difference in the world and this war.

"Nope. I won't let you wimp out. It's civvies night tonight and there's a band. The place is going to be packed and crawling with eligible man-flesh all sporting muscular thighs in shorts or nice butts in really tight jeans."

After a lifetime spent in cammies or flight suits, civvies night was something to stir the excitement at camp.

Carrie let out a breath that was half-laugh, half-sigh of resignation. "Alright. Just let me throw on some clothes." Some clothes that wouldn't be sweltering hot in the open air, un-air conditioned, and probably crowded bar.

Her clothing choices being pretty limited since ninety percent of her wardrobe consisted of desert camouflage uniforms or tan flight suits, it took her about five minutes to throw on khaki shorts and an olive drab tank top, run her hands through her still damp but rapidly drying hair, and throw on some lip gloss, more because her lips felt chapped and less for the beauty aspect.

Less than ten minutes later, Lawanda and she approached the noise and lights that announced the nearness of their destination and all too soon Carrie walked hesitantly for the first time into what was known on camp as *The Cantina.*

Carrie's glance swung to take in the crowd, feeling so out of her element she couldn't imagine what had possessed her to come tonight. No, that was wrong. She knew why she had come. It was because when the one and only woman who had been nice to her had invited her to come, she didn't dare say no. An invitation like this might never come again, and six months living among women who never talked to you was simply too long.

So here Carrie was, out at nearly twenty-one hundred hours in a crowded, smoky, loud bar instead of sleeping in her rack, and if she knew what was good for her, she'd pretend to enjoy it. Although, when Lawanda approached a table full of the same women who had ignored Carrie so effectively since her arrival at camp, she had to wonder if this little jaunt had been a huge mistake.

Steeling her nerves, she pasted on a friendly smile and greeted them all after Lawanda thrust her at the group. She supposed now she'd have to stay for at lest an hour or appear rude for leaving, but damn, she would far rather be sleeping.

There were no seats left at the table and the bar was getting increasingly crowded by the minute. Carrie felt more and more out of place as Lawanda perched her butt on the edge of one of the other women's chairs as she herself stood awkwardly near the table.

"Hey. Let me get the first round," Carrie offered. At least going up to the bar would give her something to do.

"Hey, hey! I knew I liked you!" Lawanda said, digging

into the plastic holder behind the ID card hung from a lanyard around her neck. “Let me give you my beer card.”

Carrie frowned. “Beer card?”

“Jeez, you weren’t lying. You really aren’t a big drinker, are you? There’s a three-beer limit on camp. They keep track with the cards. Just hand that to the bartender for my beer and he’ll mark it off.”

“I guess that means you don’t have a beer card for yourself. If you plan on drinking you better ask your OIC for one real soon cause I’m not giving up one of my three to you,” one of the women at the table said nastily, handing over her own card. Carrie thought the less than friendly female’s name was Cindy. At least, that is what the tattoo on the top of her prominently displayed breast read.

She only noticed the tattoo after she got past the dark brown roots in the middle of Cindy’s bleached blonde hair. She must have run out of hair dye and the PX didn’t have any in stock, or something like that. In any case, it made for an unfortunate skunky look.

Wrenching her mind away from pondering why any woman would try to maintain dyed hair while deployed, Carrie got back to the original beer discussion. “That’s fine. I was going to drink water tonight anyway.”

She honestly wasn’t really a drinker and she definitely did not want any favors from bleached, booby-baring Cindy here. Aside from Lawanda, Carrie would be happy if they never bothered to speak to her again, but it would be nice if they didn't shoot her nasty looks when she walked by. Besides, Carrie knew she should be drinking water tonight anyway. She still felt dehydrated from her PT with Beau that evening. The day had been an extra hot scorcher and it didn't help that they talked the entire run.

The three other women seated at the table with Lawanda and Cindy handed her three more beer cards and Carrie felt relieved she'd thought to throw a second twenty-dollar bill into her pocket as an afterthought. She had no clue how much beers cost. But hopefully a cold beer would buy their happiness and thaw out the chilly conditions among these particular females. That would be worth it, whatever the price.

The Cantina was so crowded, getting close to the bar was a challenge in itself. Civvies night was a big deal when you lived in a uniform seven days a week, and the camp had turned out to celebrate en masse. Standing on tiptoe, Carrie had just shouted her order for five beers and one bottle of water when she heard near her ear a familiar voice that sent a small shiver down her spine in spite of the stifling heat and crowd.

"Well, well, well. Fancy seeing you here."

She turned to find Beau smiling behind her, looking

scrumptious. She'd seen him out of uniform when they ran in their PT shorts and t-shirts, but they were both drenched in sweat each time. Tonight he was dressed in knee-length khaki cargo shorts, clean sneakers with short white socks, and a white collared golf shirt that set off his tanned skin nicely.

He was so close that over the mingled stench of spilt beer, oppressively hot air, and too many bodies, Carrie could still detect a light whiff of pine-scented soap on his skin. She couldn't resist thinking that Beau cleaned up real nice.

She returned his smile while forcing to the back of her overactive imagination the vision of Beau not only out of his uniform, but also out of his civvies, possibly lying in her bunk.

Mmm, mmm. A girl could dream, couldn't she?

"You look nice," she grinned.

His smile widened. "Thanks. I'm not much of a clothes shopper. One of my sisters gave me the shirt for my last birthday. So, I've never seen you here before. I was under the impression you didn't come to the Cantina."

Just then the bartender yelled to her how much the beers were. By her calculations, they came to a dollar fifty each. Too bad she wasn't a drinker. This place was a bargain. Alan would be thrilled, except for the three-beer limit, that is. But were he here, he could use her beer card, too, and have six all to himself.

Feeling homesick again and wishing her friend were here to ward off the sting of the bitchy women, she handed the bartender a twenty and received the newly marked beer cards in exchange.

Turning back to Beau and his previous comment, she said, “I don’t usually come here. In fact, this is the first time. My neighbor dragged me.”

Carried hooked a thumb back at the table full of women and Beau followed her gaze. “Ah,” he said simply.

The tone of his voice caught her attention immediately.

“*Ah*, what?” she asked, very interested in knowing what he was thinking but had not said.

He shrugged. “Nothing. I just know the blonde one is all.”

Cindy?

Was this jealousy rearing its ugly head when Carrie thought about Beau *knowing* Cindy? Carrie felt her brows shoot up as she wondered exactly how, but more importantly *how well* Beau knew *the blonde one*.

What little Carrie had gleaned from living with the other woman had left her with the impression that Cindy was not a very nice girl, apparently in any respect.

Carrie forced herself to sound casual. “Really? That

sounds ominous."

Beau laughed. "Ominous. Yeah, I guess you could use that word. It's no big deal. Some women can't handle their alcohol as well as others, I guess." He shrugged like it was no big deal.

The bartender chose that moment to start passing the bottles of beer and water to her as she struggled to juggle them all. Beau immediately reached over and took four bottles from her, each of his large hands easily holding two, leaving Carrie with one beer and her water.

"Speaking of women handling their alcohol, these aren't all for you, I assume, since there is a three beer limit." He grinned.

Carrie shook her head and held the water up. "Nope. This is for me. The rest are for them. I figure I'll win their hearts through bribery and alcohol."

Beau waited for her to get her change, leave a tip on the wet, beer splattered surface and then make her way around the patrons crushing toward the bar in search of beverage before he asked with a frown, "Are those girls giving you trouble?"

She shrugged. "Not really. It's just that they're not the most welcoming bunch when it comes to newcomers, except for Lawanda. She's the one that invited me to come tonight."

They'd reached the table and Carrie noted the diverse looks on the faces of its inhabitants. Lawanda was grinning widely. Cindy's eyes were narrowed with what could only be described as pure hatred and her cronies displayed various degrees of interest and judgment.

Carrie handed Lawanda the one beer she held while Beau distributed the rest, amid various raised and overly-plucked eyebrows.

Trying to ignore the reaction, Carrie said, "This is Staff Sergeant Adams. He's crew chief. I've gone up with his crew in the CH-53 a few times."

That was the absolute truth, so why did the looks get even more expressive, or perhaps suggestive?

She heard one woman whisper nastily to another, "I bet that's not all they've done."

Her eyes immediately flew to Beau's face to see if he'd heard the comment. Judging by the sudden hard set of his jaw, Carrie guessed he'd heard, all right. When he responded to the remark, it left no doubt. She could be certain, he had heard. The only question was, what would he do in response?

He stared directly at the offending party. "You're right. Tech Sergeant Armstrong pretty much kicks my butt out on the run trail every evening after work. The way she can run, I wouldn't be a bit surprised to find out she's won the

Marine Marathon one day."

Carrie appreciated his trying, but it seemed like the more he defended her, the more the women at the table looked convinced they were having sex. She sighed. Oh, well. It wasn't like they were her friends or anything. No loss. But the faster she got Beau moving and on his way, the better.

Turning toward him, Carrie said, "Thanks for helping me carry the beers, Beau." The last word had barely crossed her lips when she realized her error and cringed.

The minute his first name had left her mouth, she regretted it. Hoping no one had noticed how informally she'd addressed him was a lost cause as shocked silence fell over the women at the table.

Carrie was grateful when Lawanda finally broke the tension by raising her bottle in a salute to him. "Yeah, thanks for the beer, Staff Sergeant Adams." She emphasized his rank and name teasingly, but at least her smile seemed genuine, unlike the others at the table.

Beau shook his head to correct Lawanda. "Nuh, uh. Carrie bought y'all the beers, I just helped carry 'em. And now I have to go and get one for my friend over there before he thinks I up and left him. Have a good night, ladies. Carrie."

He nodded his good bye to the table, adding a private

look and nod for her. The glance he shot her before turning and leaving told her he had her back if she needed it. Carrie appreciated the sentiment but no man could truly understand the viciousness women could inflict upon each other. However Carrie, on the other hand, had a feeling she was about to taste it full force.

"So…" Cindy began after slurping at her longneck bottle.

"So?" Carrie acted dumb, playing with a drip of condensation that rested on her fingertips.

Lawanda sat forward eagerly. "So tell us about you and the helicopter hottie over there."

Carrie frowned and cracked open her water. "There's nothing to tell. His run buddy got hurt, that other Marine he's sitting with over there, so I've been running with him."

Cindy raised a brow and glanced at Crash. "He doesn't look too hurt to me."

"It's shin splints. He's not really hurt-hurt." Why did she feel the need to defend herself to this bitch? Even thinking that unflattering word about another female was against Carrie's nature, but in this case, it fit.

"Hmm. Well, I'm sure he's after more than a running partner." It seemed even Carrie's buddy Lawanda was getting into the act.

Carrie sighed deeply and seriously considered leaving.

But to do that would leave them alone to gossip at will and she'd be damned before she did that, especially since there was nothing to gossip about. "There is nothing going on. We run, we come back. That's it."

"I'm sorry, honey. I didn't mean to insinuate anything. It's just that if I were with that hot man every day getting sweaty, I would want it to be from doing something other than running." Lawanda took another swig of beer and waggled her eyebrows suggestively.

As annoyed as Carrie was at the rest of them, she couldn't help but laugh at Lawanda's lust as she glanced over her shoulder just as Beau carried two beers over to the table where Crash sat.

"Yeah, well, it's not like that. He's never hinted at anything like that and even if he did, I wouldn't take him up on it."

Cindy suddenly went from looking pissed off to being very interested. "Why is that? You swing the other way?" Cindy elbowed her neighbor. "See. I told you I thought she might be a lesbian!"

Maybe Carrie should say yes. At least that would end the rumor about her and Beau, but it would just open up a whole other can of worms. Besides, she didn't take to lying.

"No, I'm not a lesbian. I just don't believe in mixing work and romance. He and I have to work together. I've gone up with his crew three times already in the past week and a half. Things would be awkward if we were anything more than just co-workers or friends."

Besides the fact it was against the rules, although these women didn't look the type to worry about rules.

"Honey, we're not talking romance! We're talking fucking. Pure and simple."

Carrie laughed again at Lawanda's honestly. "Yeah, well, it's the same thing for me."

Lawanda shook her head as her eyes landed on a tall, muscular, chocolate-skinned Navy Seabee who had turned and given her the eye. "Mmm, mmm. Look at that. I sure am glad I'm not burdened by your morals, girl. Excuse me while I go get me a taste of some of that."

With Lawanda off in search of love, or whatever, Carrie made her excuses, sure at least that Cindy would be relieved to be rid of her anyway. Without even stopping to say goodnight to Beau, Carrie slunk gratefully back to her cube, alone but vowing that this would be her last girl's night out.

Chapter Five

After that night at the Cantina, where he had witnessed first hand how some of the women on camp treated Carrie, Beau made it his business to watch out for her.

Maybe it was having grown up with sisters, but he felt very protective of this woman. Finding her routinely sitting and eating alone in the chow hall, or learning through some casual comment she let drop that she had spent the night in her cube alone reading a book because the women in her tent wouldn't give her the time of day, just plain pissed him off.

Particularly that Cindy woman.

Beau prided himself on being a southern gentleman usually, and he didn't use derogatory terms for a female lightly, but he could think of a few that applied in Cindy's case. That is why it was with particular though mean-spirited pleasure that he very pointedly and obviously bypassed the table where Cindy and her friends sat.

Beau barely acknowledged the woman, in spite of her perky greeting and he ignored the empty seat next to her as he instead worked a meandering path all the way to the very back of the dining hall to sit opposite Carrie at her table.

She glanced up, smiled at him and asked, "What are you grinning so big about?"

Beau felt silly admitting his pettiness. "Nothing. It's stupid."

"Come on. I could use a good laugh."

From the weary look on her face, he bet she could. Poor thing, stuck living with those judgmental women. It would be like sleeping in a nest of vipers night after night.

Beau said a silent thank you that he'd been born a man, for so many reasons.

"It's just, you should have seen the look on Cindy's face when I didn't sit at her table. I walked right past her and came and sat with you."

Carrie rolled her eyes. "Thanks. That should make things even more friendly back at my tent."

Beau groaned. "I know, but you shouldn't have to put up with that shit from them. I am sorry, though, Carrie. I probably did make it worse for you."

"It's okay. I just can't figure out why she hates me so much. I've never done anything to her. The only time she even looked near to being nice to me was when she asked if I was a lesbian."

Beau's ears perked up at the same time that his heart sank. No! Carrie couldn't be...could she?

The part of Beau's brain which was into self-denial asked why did he care if she was or wasn't? They were just friends, and he could still be a friend and a coworker with her no matter what her sexual orientation. The other part of Beau's psyche, the one ruled by parts lower, cared a great deal.

Carrie continued, unaware of Beau's inner dialogue. "Then the minute I told her I wasn't a lesbian, Cindy was back to being her good old nasty self."

He said yet another silent thank you as she went on.

"And what really gets me is she and her friends keep hinting stuff about you and me, just because we run together. It's ridiculous. You know?"

Beau sighed. This was exactly what he'd been afraid of when Crash first suggested they run together, only he assumed it would be his guys doing the teasing with him as the target. He never imagined the women would torture Carrie so.

"Listen. I don't want you having to deal with this just because we go running every day. If you want to stop PT-ing together…" Beau suggested.

"No!" she interrupted him before he even finished the sentence.

Her fervor took him aback. "Okay. I just thought it might help the situation with the other women. That's fine. I don't want to stop running with you, either." And it had nothing to do with Crash still being laid up with shin splints.

Beau took a deep breath as he decided to confess the truth to her. "Look, Carrie, I have to tell you something. I think the reason she's being such a bitch to you might have something to do with me."

His eyes dropped briefly to the plate in front of him. When he glanced up again, it was to find Carrie looking at him warily.

"What does Cindy being mean to me have to do with you?" she asked.

Beau glanced around to make sure no one was listening. He drew in a lungful of air and steeled himself to tell the sordid tale he would rather forget.

"The week after I arrived she was real drunk one night at the Cantina. She came on to both Crash and me. We said no, of course."

Beau wanted that point made perfectly clear. Even though it was obvious the girl was willing to take on both him and Crash at the same time if they were willing, that was not a party for three Beau wanted in on.

He lowered his voice further. "Anyway, one of the guys who had been here awhile had already told us how she gets more rides than the carousel at the county fair, so when she got annoying, we ditched her with a couple of soldiers who looked interested and figured that was it. But then when I got back to my cube later, she was in there, passed out, naked on my bed."

Carrie's hazel eyes couldn't have opened any wider without her eyeballs popping out. "Oh my god. What did you do?"

"I didn't touch her, that's for damn sure! I went and got my OIC and told him that some girl we'd seen drunk at the Cantina had wandered into my tent by mistake and passed out in my bed. I didn't mention that she'd most likely gone there on purpose hoping to score with me and Crash."

Carrie looked relieved at the information that he hadn't touched Cindy. He was pretty relieved himself at his foresight and wise choice during that awkward episode. It possibly saved him from a shit load of possibly career-ending trouble.

Wide eyed, Carrie commented, "You got your OIC?

Uh, oh. I bet that wasn't pretty."

He let out a disgusted laugh. "Yeah. It wasn't pretty. My OIC went and got her OIC and brought him back to my cube. That was about the time she woke up and found all of us in there staring at her passed out and naked and she was not real happy about it, I can tell you that."

Carrie stifled a giggle but still looked pretty shocked when she asked, "Did you end up getting into trouble?"

"Hell no. I mean I hadn't done anything wrong, not that that always gets you off the hook, but lucky for me enough people saw her getting drunker and drunker at the Cantina. One Marine even saw her stumbling toward my tent alone about an hour before I left the bar. And I had witnesses. I left with a bunch of my guys and went to the chow hall to grab a sandwich before bed. That, and the fact I told my commander the minute I found her and I had Crash to back me up helped. But she got into a bit of trouble."

"What happened to her?" Carrie leaned forward, eager for more dirt on Cindy. Beau didn't blame her one bit.

"I'm not sure if she got written up or not. I think they tend to let the first time pass with a warning, but she wasn't allowed in the Cantina for two weeks after that. And the bartenders on duty got into deep shit for serving her when she was obviously drunk, besides the fact they most likely served her more than three beers unless she's a real light weight when it comes to drinking."

Carrie shook her head, looking amazed. "Wow. I don't know what to say." Then she broke out in a grin. "Boy oh boy, Beau Adams, I never ever thought being friends with you would cause me so much trouble."

The truth of her words hit him square between the eyes. Beau's guilt that he was the reason for her problems with Cindy totally outweighed his happiness over the fact that he and Carrie had indeed become friends in the past few weeks.

"I know. I am really sorry about causing you trouble," he apologized with absolute sincerity.

"No. Don't be sorry. Are you crazy? I was only kidding. Believe me. I would rather have you as my friend than all five of them. Lawanda has a good heart, but besides her, those other four women aren't looking out for anybody but themselves."

"I'm looking out for you. Don't forget that." Without hesitation, Beau reached out and let his hand cover hers.

He watched her eyes soften. "Thanks. That means a lot."

Then he realized how their hands clasped across the chow table would look, particularly to Cindy and her crew, and he drew back quickly and worked on concentrating his full attention on his food.

Embarrassed over his own lapse in judgment, he would have been happy to remain silent for the remainder of the meal, but Carrie had other ideas. Today, she was suddenly chatty.

"So I haven't seen you around all day. Where have you been hiding?"

It was just a casual question. Wasn't it? Beau tried to shake out of his head the idea that Carrie had noticed he was missing because she had been looking for him. Stupid. Why would she be looking for him? They had today's run time already set up from the day before.

Chastising himself for seeing things where there was nothing to be seen, he shoved the silly idea out of his mind and answered the question. "I've been in the damn theater all morning for a safety stand down."

The required safety stand down. What a waste of time that little military tradition was. Beau had been in the Marines long enough to not need the safety refresher course that was routinely and far too often forced upon them all. But that was the military for you, dotting all the 'i's and crossing all the 't's twice, just to make sure.

She groaned in sympathy. "Ugh. That sucks."

As he nodded in agreement, an unbidden image flashed through Beau's mind. Him. Carrie. The darkened theater full of troops watching the safety movie. Carrie's hand straying to his thigh, then creeping upwards to find his cock hard and ready for her touch. The knowledge that they could do quite a bit there in the dark and no one would be the wiser. And with that vision, his dick was hard, right there in the chow hall, and he felt his face heat.

Beau scooted his chair further under the table and considered where the hell that thought had come from. He liked Carrie. He respected her, both as an Airman and as a person. So why was he suddenly picturing her pretty little mouth wrapped around his erection.

Shit. That image did not help his ever-growing situation one little bit.

Carrie was a competent SatCom operator and a nice person but above all else she was a woman—a hot, sexy, intelligent, beautiful female and he knew it, as much as he pretended not to notice.

Lucky for Beau, Carrie was content to keep on talking to him while he worked on talking his dick into deflating before it embarrassed him any further. Beau's sole goal was to finish this meal and get the hell out of that chow hall and away from the suddenly tempting Carrie.

But as the shrill sound of sirens erupted, Beau realized that wasn't meant to be.

Loudspeakers throughout camp sprang to life. *"Attention on the camp! Attention on the camp! This is not a drill. This is not a drill. All personnel report to the nearest bunker. I say again, all personnel report to the nearest bunker. Vehicle borne IED threat. Vehicle borne IED threat."*

Beau did not hesitate. Without another thought, he grabbed Carrie's hand and pulled her from her seat, dragging her around the table and out of the door of the dining hall. Together, along with everyone else in their vicinity, they ran to the nearest bunker. It was nothing more than a concrete reinforced rectangle of a building, but it was the safest place to be at the moment, particularly if the announcement was correct and a truck full of explosives had breached the perimeter and was on its way inside.

"What's happening?" Carrie cried when they'd reached the bunker. "We're supposed to be among friendlies. Who would want to bomb us?"

Beau instinctively ran his hand up and down Carrie's back in an unconscious effort to calm her. Half of his brain realized he shouldn't be touching her so intimately in public, while the other half couldn't stop.

"It doesn't matter where we are, darlin'. All it takes is one insane person who wants to die a martyr. You've been in the military long enough to know that."

Beau felt Carrie trembling beneath his hand and he suddenly didn't give a shit who saw them standing so closely together, touching. She was scared and needed him right then, and that was all that mattered to him. Then he realized something that he'd never considered before. Maybe Carrie had never been stationed outside of the continental United States before.

Gently, he asked, "Carrie, is this your first time OCONUS?"

Defensively, she replied, "No. I was in Korea, Japan and Germany."

Beau sighed. None of which was Iraq, or Afghanistan or even Djibouti. He pulled her closer in a one-armed half hug. "Don't worry. We'll be fine here in the bunker. I promise you that."

He hesitated but finally removed his hand from her before someone noticed his touch and the rumors began to really fly. But the worst part was, he really didn't want to stop touching her once he had started.

Shit. She felt far too good in his arms. He had to get away from her and soon. Unfortunately, he had a bad feeling physically distancing himself from Carrie wasn't going to be enough.

The next day Beau decided to hit the camp gym.

Although the details of the prior day's events were

sketchy, as the higher-ups never handed out information easily, it was clear the IED had never exploded.

So why did Beau still feel shaken to the core? Unfortunately, that was clear, also. It was the damn feelings for Carrie that had assaulted him during the threat and hadn't let up since. He wanted to protect her, hold her, and much, much more.

Beau figured some good old weight lifting would clear his head. Lately, the only exertion he'd gotten was running with the very person who filled his head, the very same reason his mind needed clearing out.

He went in to the gym thinking that maybe pumping some iron until his muscles gave out would make him so exhausted he wouldn't have to pump his own dick in order to finally fall asleep that night.

Beau felt his face flush when he recalled the images of himself and Carrie that had filled his mind the night before as, worked up from his run with her, he went into the shower trailer, thankfully found it empty and proceeded to snap his bean, as all the Marines on camp liked to call the very popular extracurricular activity.

Throwing his towel and bottle of water on the floor next to the weight bench, he lay down and slowly hoisted the heavily loaded weight bar up into the air, holding it there for a second before lowering it steadily down toward his chest.

Slow and steady. Up and down. This mantra, repeated silently in his head, worked for a few reps, and then slowly it morphed into something else. *In and out. Carrie beneath him. Tight and wet. Her breath in his ear, crying out his name as he felt her body contract while she came, her muscles gripping him deep inside her.*

"Shit," he said beneath his breath, abandoning the weight to sit up before anyone noticed the rapidly growing tent in his shorts.

Running his hands over his face, Beau realized he couldn't go on like this much longer. Each day he denied himself satisfaction, the real kind, not the kind he provided himself, the urge got stronger.

So what should he do? Hook up with some random drunken female at the Cantina and get it out of his system? There was always one or two who glanced suggestively his way, if not openly flirted, or in the case of Cindy (whom he would rather forget about) literally threw herself naked at him. But that wasn't his style, on top of being far too risky. He wasn't going to risk his career for some random snatch at pussy.

Besides all that, Beau had a really bad feeling that this longing wouldn't go away from having sex with a substitute rather than the woman who, for better or worse, recently occupied his thoughts so often. And Carrie was not the kind of woman you fucked for a night and forgot about, which disturbed him even more. She was the kind of girl who threatened your bachelor status without even knowing she was doing it, which was maybe the most endearingly attractive thing about her.

He sighed, grabbed the towel, and rubbed it over his face and head hard, trying to erase the thoughts that wouldn't let his mind rest.

"Hey. Fancy seeing you here."

The familiar voice cut through directly to his core. Glancing up Beau saw Carrie, her athletic body clad in workout clothes, smiling down at him.

"Hey there. What are you doing at the gym? You're a runner at heart." Beau dropped the towel so it lay across his lap, just in case he needed the coverage in that area.

She shrugged. "Man, or woman, can't live by cardio alone. I like to strength train twice a week. I'm surprised I haven't seen you here before."

And there went Beau's last idea for a place where he could get away from the temptation that was Carrie, not that it had worked all that well today since she apparently followed him around inside his head no matter where he went or what he did. She didn't have to be there physically to haunt his dreams as well as his waking hours.

"Yeah. I used to come every day when we first arrived.

I kind of got out of the habit recently, especially since you have been kicking my ass on the run trail every day."

She pursed her lips and looked contrite. "I'm sorry. That's my fault. If you want to take a few days off a week from running to work out here instead, I'll totally understand. I can run alone."

"No." Beau realized that sounded a little too enthusiastic and added quickly, "It's good for me. Running with you forces me into doing it. I don't want to get out of the habit. I tend to get real lazy when it comes to running if I don't do it every day."

He didn't mention that until Carrie's appearance in his life, he had positively loathed running.

Beau thought briefly of the other habit, that solo activity, he'd gotten into doing every day since he'd started running with Carrie. Not much chance he'd break that one, either. Lucky for him, she was not a mind reader.

He looked up from where he straddled the weight bench to see Carrie looking suddenly uncertain as she dug her sneaker-covered toe into the floor. "Um, did you hear? There's a bus trip into town tonight. A bunch of the girls are going."

She made eye contact and then quickly looked away again. "I wouldn't mind seeing the town of Djibouti, but I really don't want to go with them, and there's that rule about sticking together when off camp. You, uh, don't happen to be going. You know, with Crash or some of the other guys, are you?"

Now he knew why she looked so uncomfortable and felt doubly bad when he had to answer her. "No. Sorry. First of all, Crash is working nights again. He's covering for one of the guys on night shift. But besides that, none of my squad is allowed out in town. There was an, um, incident."

"An incident?" Her whole body seemed to lean closer as she teased him, "Beau Adams! You've racked up quite a bit of trouble in the short time you've been here, haven't you? What sort of *incident*?"

He felt his cheeks warm. "Well, you already know about the rule that we all have to stick together when we're off camp and on leave out in town, for safety reasons."

She nodded.

"Well, the first trip my squadron made into town, one idiot got drunk and went off on his own. No one noticed right away, and when we did discover he was gone there was an all out search for him."

Her brow rose with interest as she asked, "So where did you find him?"

This part was not going to be easy to tell to a woman, particularly an innocent one like Carrie.

"With a…um…French hooker." He rushed on, "The

guy was lucky we found him, too, because those hookers will rob you faster than they'll f..." Beau felt his face color and stopped himself from finishing the thought.

Carrie's eyes opened wide. "A French hooker? Really? Wow. So what happened to the guy? Did he get into big trouble?"

"The CO who was out with us got into a big heap of shit for not noticing the guy was missing right away and then he made sure that every Marine in my squadron had all future leaves to Djibouti cancelled for the remainder of our stay here."

She giggled softly at that. Her face lit up so brightly with her smile and looked so beautiful that his eyes stalled briefly on her before he managed to drag them away and back down to his towel-draped lap.

"I bet you all never let that one Marine forget that he ruined it for everyone," Carrie continued talking, not having any clue the effect she had on him.

"Hmm? Oh, yeah. You can say that again. But still, fact is, I can't go with you tonight and I'm really sorry."

The truth was, Beau felt relieved he couldn't go. Going into town with Carrie would feel, and look to others, too much like a date. Besides, the way his mind was going today, he couldn't risk being alone in that kind of atmosphere with her. He'd embarrass himself for sure.

"That's alright. There's nothing I needed to see out in town, anyway. French hookers aren't really my thing." She shrugged and made the lame joke as if it didn't matter if she went or not, but that wasn't true at all.

Beau's heart broke for her because he knew it did matter, a lot. From what he had seen, most of the women were absolute raving bitches to Carrie. It hurt her, he could tell, and for better or worse that, in turn, hurt him.

This intelligent, beautiful, kind woman spent every night in her cube, friendless, bored, and alone. And now, when there arose one small opportunity for fun and diversion, she wouldn't go because he couldn't.

Worse, even though he tried, Beau couldn't even begin to comprehend the loneliness she must be feeling. How could he? He and Crash had been with one another for years, both on deployments and when stationed Stateside.

They'd even had a pretty nice stint in Hawaii together. Drinking beers and surfing in their off hours. Those months had been the most fun Beau had had in years. But he couldn't imagine being this far from home for such a long deployment while feeling as totally alone and friendless as Carrie obviously did.

But she wasn't really friendless. Beau was her friend, even if his lower extremities had other ideas for the two of them. He sighed and before he knew it, he was doing something about her sadness. He bumped her leg with his shoulder and said, "Hey."

She glanced down at him with interest. "Yeah?"

"You wanna do something tonight here on camp?" The minute the words were out, he regretted them, until he noted that Carrie looked more cheerful instantly.

She seemed to stand up straighter and her voice sounded almost perky. "Okay. Like what?"

He pushed what he would like them to do together immediately out of his mind and said, "I don't know. We could watch a movie, I guess. I've got some DVDs and a TV in my office. Or we could go to the Cantina. With Cindy and her friends gone, you might actually enjoy it this time."

He'd seen her leave almost right away that one night after those women made that nasty comment about the two of them. With that memory, the stupidity of this idea for them to do something alone together hit him square between the eyes.

He should not be spending more time with Carrie. There was already talk about them getting inappropriately close and though previously unfounded, now, apparently, he was interested in her personally, or more accurately physically.

But she had looked so sad and lonely before, he argued

with himself, and now, she was actually excited.

"Okay. Anything you want to do is fine. Your choice. I don't care." That was so not what he needed her to say at the moment.

She smiled and his heart started to pound.

Beau swallowed hard. "I'll think about it and let you know at our run later."

"Great." Then she hesitated. "Wait. Do you still want to run after your workout here?"

He nodded, having a feeling that his workout here was done and unwilling to give up that private time with her. Beau had gotten far too used to their nightly ritual over the past weeks.

"Yeah, I still want to if you do."

Her smile broadened. "Of course I do. Wouldn't miss it."

He smothered a sigh as the pile of shit he was in got a little bit deeper.

Just great.

Chapter Six

"Ooh Rah! You and Sergeant Hocakes. Way to go!" Crash waggled his eyebrows suggestively.

"I should have never mentioned this to you." Beau resisted the urge to kick something, possibly Crash, with his well-worn size ten and a half combat boot.

"Too bad. It's too late. You did mention it and there's nothing you can do about it now," Crash challenged. "So what are you gonna do with her? Not that there are a hell of a lot of options for things to do around here, but where are you thinking of taking her?"

"Hell if I know." He'd been wracking his brain with that exact question since he'd made the crazy offer. And now he was supposed to be meeting her for their run and tell her what they'd be doing later that night and he still had no clue.

Beau paced the floor of the office to finally land in front of Crash's desk as he accused, "This is all your fault, you know."

"My fault! Why is it my fault? You made the damn date."

"It's not a date," he growled. "And you are the one who put the damn idea in my head to begin with. Saying she was a hocakes and that shit about how I needed to get laid."

With his hands rubbing back and forth over his shorn hair in frustration, Beau searched for the right words. "It's like you planted the suggestion deep in my brain and now I suddenly can't look at her without picturing her naked."

Crash cocked one brow and asked in surprise, "And that's a bad thing? Anyhow, it doesn't sound like she agreed to get naked with you no matter what you are picturing deep in that pea brain of yours, so don't fret about it. Remember, she's the camp ice queen so you're worrying for nothing."

And wasn't that the ironic part? Cindy and her friends hated Carrie because they assumed she slept around, or at least, that she was doing so with Beau. And the men all called Carrie Ice Queen because they assumed she never would.

And all of that, in a nutshell, was the reason people

should not make assumptions. There was definitely something to that old saying *when you assume…*

"You make an ass out of you and me," Beau completed the phrase out loud with a soft mumble.

"What?" Crash frowned at him.

Beau shook his head. "Nothing. Just thinking."

But Crash was right. Just because he'd taken a turn for the gutter, didn't mean Carrie had suddenly lost her morals. She didn't sleep around and just because Beau sometimes, okay, often, thought of her naked, didn't mean she'd start now.

Which brought him back to his original dilemma, what to do with her.

Beau went back to his pacing. It helped him think about his stupidity. "When I made this asinine suggestion in the first place, I said we would maybe watch a DVD or go get a few beers. But I've been rethinking that plan."

"Why? Sounds good to me." Crash shrugged.

"Cause I don't know that I want anyone here at camp to see us together like that. There's talk already and all we've done is run and grab chow together. The other guys in the shop will see us if we're in here watching a movie. You know there will be comments made about that. And we sure as hell can't watch a DVD on my laptop in either one of our cubes. That would really start the tongues wagging."

"Simple. It's the Cantina then," Crash said.

There was no way anything about this situation was simple. Beau groaned. "No. Are you crazy? You know the Cantina is just one big rumor mill."

Crash looked annoyed. "Well, since you don't have a better idea, what are you gonna do with her?"

"Shit. I already told you. I'll be damned if I know. But I have to come up with something. I promised and now she is all excited."

Crash raised his eyebrows again suggestively.

"Shut up." Beau cut him off before he even opened his mouth, this time with some crude comment about Carrie being "excited".

Crash threw his hands up in the air defensively. "Hey! I didn't say a word."

"Keep it that way."

After a too brief moment of silence, Crash said, "Am I allowed to make a suggestion for your…ah…evening?"

"Don't you dare call it a date," Beau ordered.

"I didn't. I called it an *evening.* You sure it isn't a date?" Crash smirked.

"No! I mean, yes, I'm sure. It's not a date." He stared Crash right in his beady blue eyes to enforce that fact.

With a face that had doubt written all over it, Crash went on. "Fine. Whatever you say. But you still need something to do on your non-date. So here's my idea. Zippy started tending bar last week, right? Which means you can get some beers from him on the sly. There's also a band playing at the Cantina tonight. So if you take some cold beers and a blanket, you can set up in a nice secluded spot near enough to hear the music but far enough away to not be seen. Your own private concert. See?"

He hated to admit it to Crash, but he might actually have come up with a good idea, as long as they planted themselves where they wouldn't be seen.

The other thing Beau wasn't about to admit, not even to himself, was that the thought of he and Carrie on a blanket, in the dark, under the stars, was getting him worked up. It reminded him a little too much of his first time in high school all those years ago. Sneaking out of a party to be alone in the bed of his pickup truck one hot Georgia summer night. Penny Sinclair, ready and willing in her mini-skirt. Beau, more than ready to ditch his virginity…

Beau swallowed hard as he felt his dick start to get a rise at the image of Carrie beneath him instead of a teenage Penny Sinclair. Maybe this was a very, very bad idea after all.

"You coming to town with us?" Lawanda asked as she

and Carrie both emerged out of the shower trailer at the same time.

"Nah. I think I'll stay home tonight." She'd run with Beau, showered, and was now about to meet him to do something…what, she still didn't know. He'd said it was a surprise.

"Stay home? What the hell for? It's not because of Cindy and all of her stupid ass comments, is it?"

Carrie glanced at Lawanda. So there had been more comments. It wasn't just Carrie's imagination that Cindy and company were talking about her behind her back. And she'd bet a month's pay the remarks were about her and Beau.

Good to know, although what she could do about it, Carrie had no clue. But in light of the rumors, Carrie wasn't about to admit, even to Lawanda, that spending the evening there with Beau was far more enticing than a trip into the town of Djibouti with Cindy and her crew.

"Nah. It's not Cindy." She shrugged as she stretched that truth a bit.

There was another thing Carrie wasn't willing to admit, even to herself. That the last thing Carrie wanted to do was spend a night out with Cindy because the woman had, not so long ago, flirted outrageously with him before somehow winding up naked in Beau's bed.

Carrie swallowed the distaste *that* vision left in her mouth, along with the question of why it bothered her so much. Nothing had happened, or so Beau had said, but still, maybe a few more beers on his part that night and something might have.

At Lawanda's skeptical look, Carrie amended her answer. "Cindy's not *totally* the reason I'm not going, anyway. I just don't feel like it."

"Come on, it'll be fun," Lawanda prodded.

"Actually, I heard some stories that made Djibouti sound like not all that much fun after all."

"Like what kinda stories?"

"Like that the town is full of French hookers who will just as quickly rob you as...you know." Carrie caught herself before she finished the thought and blushed when she realized she'd used Beau's words nearly verbatim.

Lawanda's brows shot up. "You planning on going off with any French hookers?"

Carrie smiled. "No, of course not. But still, I don't think town is for me."

Lawanda sighed. "Okay, country girl. But if you change your mind, let me know. I grew up in the tough part of Chicago. I would take care of you if any nasty shit went down or any hookers set their sights on you."

Of that, Carrie was certain, and the knowledge that she

had at least one friend among the women made her feel better. "I know you would, Lawanda and I appreciate it. You have a great time."

Lawanda held open the flimsy wooden screen door as both of them entered their sleeping tent and said over her shoulder before popping into her cube, "Oh, I will, honey. Have no doubt."

Carrie didn't doubt it one bit. If anything was certain, it was that Lawanda could manage to have fun in any situation.

And speaking of fun…

Just thinking about hanging out with Beau that night had set Carrie's nerves on edge. Why, she didn't know. It was pretty obvious he'd asked her to do something out of guilt because he couldn't go to town with her. So why had she shaved her legs, and her bikini line, in anticipation of tonight? Just the thought that Beau might see her efforts, either or both, sent her heart racing.

She let out a long, loud, lip-flapping breath at her pointless dream. Beau treated her like a professional and as a friend, nothing more. Well, except for today when he looked at her with something more—pity. In light of that, thinking of being intimate with him was absolutely crazy.

Carrie pushed the thought out of her mind and stared at the clothes piled on the shelf of her locker. She gazed at the khaki flight suit, a stack of neatly folded black t-shirts, a few pair of desert camouflage uniform pants, one pair of jeans and one pair of khaki shorts. The rest were loose running clothes comprised of shorts and tank tops or PT t-shirts, all of which she also used to sleep in.

Perhaps this was why she was single, her woeful wardrobe. Carrie sighed. There was not a whole lot of choosing to do so she pulled down cammies and a clean black t-shirt.

Beau hadn't told her exactly what they would be doing. He said he wanted to surprise her but it didn't matter, her pitiful choice of attire would be the same no matter what he chose.

At least she wouldn't have to spend a lot of time getting ready. Although she did find herself playing more than usual with her hair as she stared in the mirror and tried not to read too much into the fact that she had felt compelled to put on both mascara and lip gloss when she rarely did either.

Dressed and ready, Carrie looked at her watch and saw she still had half an hour before she was supposed to meet Beau. She could pace back and forth within the laughably small space between the bed and her footlocker, or she could do something productive, so she pulled her laptop out of her locker and plopped down with it on her bunk. When all else failed, one could always check for email from home.

After the incredibly long and frustrating time it took the internet to connect, Carrie found an email from Alan telling her news from home and how he'd recently seen one of their old high school friends who'd moved away.

He sounded good. Real good. Maybe Carrie had been wrong. Perhaps he'd made the right choice in staying home surrounded by friends and family. Familiar surroundings. Knowing that during a trip to the market you'd likely see a good dozen people who'd known you since the day you were born, and who'd known your grandma and grandpa, too. There was something to be said for all of that.

With a sigh, Carrie hit reply and began her response.

Alan,

Things are going really great here. I've met tons of wonderful people and the work is so fulfilling. Oh, and I almost forgot. Did I tell you I saw a camel the other day while I was out running? Well, that's about it for now. Going out with friends again tonight so I better log off. Talk to you soon. Love to everyone.

Carrie

Chapter Seven

Beau arrived early at their rendezvous point and waited nervously until he saw Carrie heading toward him, and then his nerves became nearly paralyzing.

"Hey," he managed to get out by way of welcome when she was close enough to hear his soft greeting.

"Hey there." Her smile lit up her face. "So what's the plan, Mr. Secretive?"

Beau saw her eyeing the blanket in his hand. He'd grabbed it off the end of his bed. He hid beneath it the ice-cold six-pack of beer he'd gotten (against all rules) from Zippy. And if they didn't get settled and set to drinking it, it would be warm beer, he thought, feeling strangely agitated.

Beau knew damn well the temperature of their

beverages was not what really concerned him. He had drunk warm beer before and he was pretty sure he would again.

The real reason he wanted them sitting down somewhere, away from prying eyes, was that he definitely did not want anyone seeing them together and cause more talk. The interested looks they'd gotten by just chatting in the gym for a few minutes had bothered him, and reinforced how stupid his suggesting this non-date (as Crash called it) had been.

The other reason he wanted this night to get started was so it could get finished and he could get away from her before he lost his mind and did or said something he'd regret.

Glancing around to make sure no one would see them, he grabbed her hand with his free one and quickly led her to the spot he had chosen during his recon earlier. Just as Crash had suggested, it was close enough to the Cantina to hear the music from the band pumping out of the open walls once the set started, but far enough off the beaten path to be private. No security lights, only moonlight, illuminated this particular area, just as he had hoped would be the case during his daytime inspection, but it was bright enough to walk without tripping.

He stopped at the spot he'd previously selected and reluctantly dropped his hold on her hand. Putting the six-pack down on the ground, he spread the blanket out and turned to look at her. “This is it. I know it’s not much but...”

She glanced around, looking a bit confused. Then the distant sound of an announcer filled the air, followed by music.

He rushed to explain. “I figured we could have a little moonlight picnic. There’s music. Here’s some beer. Oh, and I almost forgot.” Beau reached into his pocket and pulled out a few sticks of beef jerky. He held them up for her to see in the dim light. “And appetizers.”

She smiled. “It’s perfect.”

He shook his head, regretting the idea. “No it’s not. It’s stupid. I’m sorry…”

“No. It’s not stupid. You knew exactly what I would enjoy. I love music but I don’t like crowds.” She glanced at the masses of people spilling out of the Cantina in the distance. “Thanks for doing this, Beau.”

Carrie reached out into the darkness, touched Beau’s face gently and then planted a soft kiss on his cheek.

His breath caught in his chest and he didn’t dare move for fear he would grab her and kiss her for real, the way he’d imagined. When she pulled back, he felt the immediate need to do something, so he sat on the blanket, grabbed two of the beers, and popped the tops.

Beau waited for her to sit so he could hand one to her.

"I've only ever seen you drink bottled water. You do drink beer, right?"

She giggled and folded her long legs to sit near him, too near for his comfort. "Rarely, but yeah, I've had one or two beers over the course of my lifetime."

Beau laughed. "Yeah, me, too." He'd have more like five or six a night if he had his way, but perhaps that was just the natural difference between a man and a woman.

Their hands touched for the second time that night when she took the beer, sending a spark through him, and judging by the way she pulled her hand back, through her, too.

"Jerky?" He held up one stick, desperate for something to do that wouldn't bring touching Carrie to the forefront of his over-sexed brain.

She shook her head. "No, thank you."

"You're not a vegetarian, are you?" he joked, but then searched his brain to find if he'd ever actually seen her eat meat at chow. She'd eaten the gross meatloaf the other day, hadn't she? Or was her plate filled with just mashed potatoes. Damned if he could remember.

Luckily for him, Carrie laughed and shook her head. "No, I'm not a vegetarian. I just try to keep my consumption of preservative and sodium-filled, dried meat products to a minimum."

Even though Beau considered beef jerky one of the four

major food groups, he nodded anyway. "That's probably a good plan."

In the following moment of quiet, Beau physically felt the atmosphere change between them and waited for her to speak, wondering what was up.

"Listen, Beau. I know the only reason you invited me out tonight was because you feel bad for me because of Cindy and all."

"That's not…" he began to protest.

"No. Really, it's fine. Sweet actually. I just wanted you to know that I knew why you'd asked. I'm not assuming this, tonight, is anything more than it is. Okay?"

Why did that not make him feel any better? It should be exactly what he wanted. He should be relieved. They were just friends. No misunderstandings.

"Okay," he echoed and rushed to fill the silence pressing against his disappointment. "So, tell me about home."

She let out a short laugh. "There's not much to tell. What do you want to know, exactly?"

"I don't know. Who you left behind. What it was like the day you made your decision and finally joined up. Whatever you want to tell me."

Carrie took in and released a big whoosh of air before starting to speak, and Beau was thankful it was dark out so she wouldn't notice that he couldn't resist the urge to watch the outline of her firm, high breasts rise and fall with the breath. "Well, my joining up two days after high school graduation was all part of a bet."

That amazing revelation halted his lewd thoughts right in their tracks. "What?"

She laughed. "Well, that's not exactly the entire story. I was going to enlist anyway, no matter what, but the way it ended up happening was that I joined up right after I lost a bet when I didn't win a running race against my best friend."

After having her outrun him daily for weeks, that seemed even more amazing. "You lost a race? No way. I don't believe it."

Slowly, over the course of the discussion, Carrie relaxed little by little. Beau was a good listener and easy to talk to. She relayed the entire story about her and Alan's fateful race those many years ago to him. Carrie realized that just talking about home and her old friend with her new friend made it seem like she wasn't so far away from all those she loved and who loved her. Cindy and the other women on camp seemed a world away, until it was just her and Beau, under the stars.

After finishing the story, Carrie noticed that the second beer Beau had just cracked open for her was going straight to her head. “Maybe I should have some of the jerky after all.”

“Sure thing.” He handed a stick to her in the soft filtered glow of combined moonlight and the illumination that just barely reached them from the nearest security light.

She took the beef stick and proceeded to unwrap it clumsily as he continued to speak. “I can tell you one thing. The way you push my sorry ass out on that run trail everyday, you wouldn’t lose that race today.”

Carrie laughed. “You’re right. Alan’s idea of exercise nowadays is mowing the lawn… He has a riding mower.”

Beau chuckled. “Yeah. I have a few school buddies back home who are like that. If nothing else, at least I can say the Marines kept me in good physical shape.”

“Agreed. And the Air Force paid for my education, so it’s a win-win all around.” She chewed and swallowed a bite of the tough meat product before saying, “So tell me about when you joined up.”

He shrugged. “Not much to tell there, either. There was no bet involved, I can tell you that much. I was on my way to a bar to meet a friend of mine. I passed a recruiting office and decided to stop in, just to see what kinda lies the recruiters were spouting to get guys to join up. So I walk in and some Gunny Sergeant asks me, 'What the hell do you want?' Like he was there to do me a favor. I told him I'd thought about enlisting right out of high school once but didn't, so I figured I would stop in to see what they might have to offer."

"How old were you when you went into the recruiting station this time?" she interrupted.

"I was twenty. So this crusty old Marine Gunny, who now that I think about it was probably only in his early thirties at the time, said that if pay and benefits were what I was after, then I should go elsewhere. But if I wanted to challenge myself and have some pride-of-belonging, I was in the right place."

Carrie saw Beau shrug as he looked at her from across the blanket before continuing. "That was it. I was hooked. I enlisted the next day, which didn't sit too well with my girlfriend at the time."

Carrie's heart twisted at the mention of a woman in Beau's life. "What did she do when you told her?" she asked, hoping the answer was that she broke up with him and never spoke to him again.

He laughed. "There was lots of screaming and crying. Then she got over it. I married her right after I got out of boot camp."

Carrie's crush on Beau came to a sudden heart crushing,

crashing halt. He didn't wear a ring, but still, how could she not realize he was married? That would explain why he had never ogled her the way the other men usually did.

Swallowing, she tried to make her voice sound normal and casual as she asked, "So you're married?"

When he shook his head and answered, she felt she could finally breath again. "I *was* married. The divorce has been final for a while now." He shrugged. "I guess that's what happens when you get married too young. You know?"

She nodded and made some non-committal sound of agreement, even though, having never been married, she didn't know. All she knew was that he was single now, and that was enough for her. Because even though it was wrong that she found herself attracted to him in spite of the camp rules against it, if he had been married, it would have devastated her.

Carrie could try to deny her attraction to Beau, like she had denied it to Lawanda when she had asked that night at the Cantina, and like she'd been denying it to herself for the past two weeks, but she knew she was only deluding herself. She had it bad for Beau, not just physically either, although that part was pretty intense, too. It was so much more. She enjoyed him as a friend, respected him as a leader, and really, really liked him as a man.

The band must have taken a break because the music stopped and the only sounds were those of the bar patrons having fun, laughing and talking, in the distance.

Carrie set her open half-empty beer bottle down on the blanket. “Thanks again, Beau. For tonight.”

He shifted and the blanket moved, knocking the beer over. They both reached to grab it before it soaked the fleece, and Carrie found her face in close proximity to Beau’s while her hand covered his on the now upright bottle. So close, a slight shift would bring their mouths near enough to touch.

She couldn’t bring herself to move, neither closer or further away. Heart pounding, the blood rushed audibly through her veins as her eyes dropped and she watched Beau’s throat work as he swallowed hard. And then he leaned forward, so slowly she almost felt she imagined it, until they were barely a breath apart.

There being enough beer in Carrie’s system, she did the one thing she wanted most at that time. She closed the short distance until their lips touched ever so softly. The gentleness of it brought a small sound from her throat, which elicited a low rumbling groan from deep within Beau as he grabbed the back of her neck with his hand and pressed her mouth closer against his.

She tilted her head with a soft sound as his tongue

parted her lips. He tasted of beer and jerky with an undercurrent of minty toothpaste. Her fingertips touched his cheek and she felt the freshly-shaven and wonderfully smooth skin covering the firm, strong jaw she often glanced at while they ran.

Carrie leaned in closer, wanting more of this man touching her, but then he pulled away, breaking the touch completely.

The moment was gone as quickly as it had come.

Leaning away from her, he shoved the beer bottle between his knees and scrubbed both hands over his face. "Jesus. I am so sorry, Carrie."

Carrie swallowed the lump in her throat and whispered, "Why are you sorry? I kissed you." And judging from his reaction, she had made a big mistake. "I owe you the apology."

She turned her head so he wouldn't see the tears that threatened to well up and overflow her eyes. Good thing she was well practiced at hiding her emotions.

"No. You don't owe me anything, Carrie." Beau blew out a loud breath. "Listen, it's getting late. You ready to go back?"

"Yeah. Good idea. I've got an early morning," she lied.

Beau agreed, "Yeah. Me, too."

He stood and extended his hand to help her get up.

Carrie let him assist her, figuring that this would most likely be the last time Beau Adams would willingly ever touch her again.

Chapter Eight

"So how was your non-date?" Crash smirked from across the dining hall table at lunch the following day.

Beau scowled and bit out a terse, "Fine."

"What's wrong, lover boy? Did you get shot down by the ice queen?" Crash made a pouty face before breaking out into a wide grin and Beau smothered the urge to wipe the smug look right off of him with one well-aimed fist.

That inclination made him realize his nerves had been wound far too tightly since that kiss the prior night.

"No, I didn't get shot down and you should shut the hell up. Don't call her shit like that anymore. Damn, just because a girl isn't a whore and doesn't sleep around, doesn't mean she should be ridiculed."

Beau had thought he'd been in misery before, when he'd only been picturing her and him together. Ha! That had been nothing. It was so much worse now after having tasted a bit of her. Now, after giving in to the impulse, and realizing what a bad mistake it had been, he knew what true misery felt like.

All he'd done by kissing Carrie was make their friendship awkward and uncomfortable. It reinforced in his mind how weak he was by letting himself give in to a crazy impulse and told him that they could never do it again. On top of it all, it made him want her even more and because of that, he needed to stay away from her. Far, far away.

Crash raised a brow and eyed him strangely. "Okay, Beau. Whatever you say."

He would have liked to lay into Crash, but he actually sounded sincere when he had said it, leaving Beau no excuse, and also no one to yell at to get this frustration out.

"Can you run yet?" Beau asked, looking up to see confusion written on Crash's face.

"Yeah, I think I could give it a try. Why?"

"Why the hell do you think?" He realized too late how short that had sounded. "I thought we could run together tonight."

"Fine," Crash said, and then mumbled something more as he rose from his chair to throw away his garbage and return his tray.

"What did you just say?" Beau barked.

His friend turned slowly and enunciated each and every word very clearly this time. "I said I shoulda kept my damn mouth shut to begin with."

"What's that supposed to mean?"

Crash scowled. "Think about it."

Beau didn't need to think about it to know Crash was sorry he'd ever mentioned running with Tech Sergeant Carrie Armstrong to him and Beau had to agree.

He didn't pursue this dangerous topic further and instead he called after Crash's stiff back as he walked away, "I'll meet you at the gate at seventeen-thirty for our run."

Without turning around, Crash waved one hand, which may or may not have contained an obscene gesture, in Beau's direction.

Beau sighed. If he didn't watch out, he'd go from two friends to zero friends, all over one incredible but stupid kiss.

Incredibly stupid, yup, that about covered it.

"Hey."

Beau's head whipped around at the sound of her voice, but he didn't need to see her to know it was Carrie who spoke behind him.

Heart pounding, he answered, "Hey."

She stood before him awkwardly, empty-handed. She must have just walked in, saw him sitting there alone and walked over before getting her food because he was damn sure she hadn't been in the chow hall before. He would have seen her there. No. He would have *felt* her there.

"Um. I just wanted to let you know that I have something to do later and I won't be able to run with you tonight."

His heart fell. Why, he didn't know. He'd considered backing out on her, but instead had invited Crash to act as a buffer. But to have her ditch him first, hurt. He hid that feeling and said, "That's okay. Actually, Crash is feeling better now so…"

"So you can run with him again. That's good. I mean I should probably be running alone anyway because I'm planning on starting to train for a half marathon I'm in when I get home. So, you know. It wouldn't be fair to you to make you train with me."

"Yeah. I don't do marathons," he joked, but didn't feel merry.

She turned to go but he somehow couldn't let her. "Hey, Carrie?"

"Yeah?"

"I need a SatCom Operator to go up with me for a, uh, training. Are you available?"

She hesitated slightly. “Um. I don’t know. When is it?”

“Um, tomorrow?”

“I’ll have to check with my CO.”

He had a feeling she was trying to avoid being near him, which only made him want her more. “Okay. Understood. I hope you don’t already have anything booked. I’d really like it to be you instead of someone else.”

Yeah, that didn’t sound too suggestive of other things, things that had nothing to do with satellites or communications.

Her face softened visibly. “I’ll check.”

“Good. Can you let me know when you find out?”

“Will do,” she agreed.

“Thanks.”

She hooked a thumb in the direction of the door awkwardly. “Well, I gotta go.”

Beau nodded and watched her leave the chow hall, realizing she’d never gotten anything to eat. Yeah, he’d really messed everything up last night, all right. But he was going to fix it.

He hated losing a friend, at least that was what he told himself. Deep down, he had a bad feeling that was not his real motivation, but he could think about that after he cleaned up the mess he’d made during the ill-fated moonlit beef jerky and beer picnic.

Beau waited a few minutes after she'd disappeared out of the dining hall door before dumping the half uneaten remains of his own meal and flying out into the sunlight himself.

Now for his next problem. Beau busted through the door of his shop so hard he got a dirty look from Crash. "What the hell? Is your fucking hair on fire or what?"

Worse. "I've got to get a training set up for tomorrow. And quick," Beau explained.

"Do I want to know why?" Crash asked, looking as if he suspected the reason already.

Beau shook his head. "Probably not."

No way was he telling Crash he'd just booked Carrie on a flight that didn't exist just to be near her.

Crash let out a short laugh. "You're probably right." Sighing with resignation, he offered wearily, "Sit tight. I'll see what I can do."

Beau smiled at him. "You're a good friend. You know that, Crash?"

"Yeah, I know it. Do you know it?" Crash raised one brow and waited.

Beau nodded. "Yeah, I do. And I'm not going to let myself forget it again any time soon, either."

Phone in hand, Crash said, "Good. Make sure you don't."

Minutes later, Beau paced the office as Crash made a long series of phone calls that didn't sound very promising. When Crash finally hung up, Beau halted his pacing. "Well?" he asked hopefully.

"Well, I couldn't get you a training."

"Damn." Beau ran his hand over his face. "That's okay. Thanks for trying."

"Hold on a second. I didn't get you a training, but I did get you a mission. Will that do?"

Beau laughed with relief. "Yeah, that will do."

"You're welcome," Crash said suggestively and then waited.

Beau shook his head at his smart-ass friend. "Thank you, Crash. I owe you one."

"Yeah, you do," Crash grinned.

After seeing Beau in the chow hall, Carrie lost her appetite for lunch. How could she even begin to face eating alone again after they'd shared so many meals together over the past few weeks?

Although, she would rather eat alone than with Cindy and her pack of jackals. But in the past, Beau had always ridden in and saved her from many solemn and lonely meals. It had seemed that whenever she went in to chow solo since her arrival at camp, Beau had somehow always miraculously appeared, right on cue.

But now, things would probably change. No more Beau riding to her rescue. Not after he ran away from that kiss. Although he did ask her to go up with him tomorrow. And Carrie didn't know what to make of that. All she did know was that she was suddenly looking forward to it a bit too much while at the same time she was nervous as hell about it.

Carrie was so busy thinking that she didn't see Lawanda until she literally bumped into her outside their tent.

"So how was the trip into Djibouti?" Carrie asked to cover her embarrassment.

"Well, you were right about town. There were a lot of hookers. And they don't seem to care which sex you are, either. I got a few propositions myself."

Surprised at that, Carrie laughed. "You should feel flattered, I guess."

Lawanda rolled her eyes. "Yeah, I'm sure it was because I'm so hot and had nothing to do with the fact they think Americans all walk around loaded down with cash and are too stupid to know when we're being robbed."

"Oh, well. Sorry. Did you have fun at least?"

"Yeah. I managed to and it ended up being an all right night. What did you end up doing?"

Carrie flashed back to what she'd done the night before and felt her face flush. "Um. Nothing. Hung out. You know." *Kissed Beau. Ruined our friendship. The usual.*

Lawanda shook her dark head. "You need to get out and have some fun, girl."

Carrie shrugged sadly. "Fun's overrated, Lawanda."

All that having fun had done for her so far was mess up a great relationship with Beau. She should have never invited him into town. She should not have said yes when he suggested they do something else there at camp. And she never, ever should have leaned toward him in the darkness, closed that distance between their lips and discovered how good it felt to get just a small taste of Beau Adams.

Lawanda shrugged. "To each his own, I guess. Anyway, wanna come with me to eat? I'm on my way to chow."

Lawanda's question startled her out of her memory of that kiss and reminded her that not only did she have no appetite, but also that Beau was likely still in the chow hall.

Still, she needed an excuse to not go with Lawanda.

Carrie opted for the truth, which she noticed she didn't do enough lately. "Um. No, I can't. I gotta go talk to my CO about my schedule for tomorrow."

"Cindy's not coming to lunch, if that's your problem." Lawanda dangled that piece of information in front of Carrie as temptation. Little did she know that Carrie was more intent on avoiding Beau in the dining hall than Cindy…well, maybe not more, but at least equally.

Damn, she couldn't get him out of her mind. Torn between the insane desire to see him and knowing she shouldn't because it would hurt too much, Carrie really hoped that the decision would be taken out of her hands, that she was booked up elsewhere for the following day so she wouldn't have to go up with Beau as his SatCom operator. After being so comfortable with each other for weeks, this new feeling of discomfort was very disconcerting.

"I'm not really that hungry…" Carrie began.

"Oh, come on!" Lawanda grabbed Carrie's hand and practically dragged her until she figured she better go willingly or face bodily harm.

Laughing, Carrie begrudgingly agreed. At least she had one person who still wanted to eat with her. "Okay. Okay. I'll come. Jeez! I didn't know you worried about my eating habits so much."

"It's purely selfish, trust me. I don't want to eat alone."

"Lawanda. I have never seen you eat alone, even when Cindy isn't there you usually end up surrounded by men all so busy listening to you talk they forget to eat!" Carrie reminded her.

Lawanda grinned. "Yeah, you're right. But there's

another reason for me to make sure you eat."

Carrie frowned. "What's that?"

"I figure if I get you to eat enough to put some fat on that booty of yours, some good jiggling junk in your trunk, then Cindy might quit being jealous and lay off of you. Then I can finally get some peace around this damn tent."

That knowledge stopped Carrie dead. "Cindy's jealous of me?"

"Hell yeah! You didn't know?" Lawanda looked shocked.

Glancing down at her own A-cups, Carrie asked, "Why? Next to her, I'm built like a twelve-year-old boy."

"That may be, but you've got the attention of one hot Marine crew chief, which she couldn't do."

Apparently not as much attention as everyone seemed to think, Carrie thought as she remembered Beau rushing away from the site of their one and only kiss.

Lawanda kept on talking. "That's the big thing she's jealous of. But besides that, she's put on a good fifteen pounds since she's gotten here and that drives her crazy, but no crazier than your skinny ass! It must be all that running you do that keeps you like a bean pole."

Carrie raised a brow. *A bean pole?* No wonder Beau didn't want to kiss her. "I've always naturally been on the thin side, no matter how much I eat. I can't help it."

Lawanda's eyes opened wide. "Well, Jesus. Don't tell her that! It will really make her nuts."

Carrie shook her head. If only her own worries were as ridiculous as Cindy's, she'd be in good shape. On second thought, she didn't want to be anything like Cindy and her pettiness, even if it meant keeping her own problems.

And speaking of her problems, Carrie pushed through the dining hall door holding her breath. Her gaze went immediately to Beau's table.

It was empty.

Feelings of relief and disappointment assaulted Carrie at the same time. Damn, she was going to miss his constant presence, and it was all her own fault. Her fault she kissed him. She had pushed the relationship where he didn't want it to go and made him uncomfortable.

Sadly, the knowledge she'd inflicted this pain on herself didn't make it any easier to bear.

Chapter Nine

"We'll be over the target in approximately three minutes, Staff Sergeant," the pilot informed Beau.

They communicated over a microphone built into their headsets. It connected the pilot, the copilot, the aerial observer, Beau as crew chief, and Carrie as SatCom operator on this mission.

Crash hadn't been able to arrange a bogus training, but he had talked his ass off in order to arrange taking the bird up on a goodwill mission today, rather than later in the week.

Crash had really hooked him up when he somehow managed to get the date moved and get both Beau and Carrie assigned to the thing last minute. The man was amazing at pulling strings, juggling schedules and arranging things just the way he wanted them, all while making others think it was their own idea.

It was a pretty incredible feat, and a lot to ask of his friend, but Beau was determined. He had to get things back to normal with Carrie, even if normal meant just friends. Having this mission as an excuse for them to work together again could only help his cause and show her that things could be the same as before, as long as she let them.

Of course, Beau wasn't so sure he wanted things the same as before himself. But that was a thought for later. Now, he had a job to do.

"Copy that," Beau responded to the pilot. "Tech Sergeant Armstrong, make ground contact."

"Roger that, Staff Sergeant." The communicator funneled Carrie's voice directly into his ear, sending a chill down his spine even though she hadn't said anything even remotely personal.

Carrie contacted the troops on the ground. "They're ready down below."

"Good to go. Lower the ramp and let 'em go!" Beau ordered.

"Ramp lowered." The AO shoved the load of soccer balls off the ramp of the CH-53 over an open field near the Djiboutian orphanage. Beau watched the cargo net dangling as it drifted slowly to the ground beneath the parachute.

The package had barely touched down when they saw children streaming out of the building and running toward the toys. Beau smiled, glad he'd been there to witness the drop off of the balls donated by a corporation back in the States.

Glancing up, Beau could observe, unnoticed, as Carrie smiled while she, too, watched the scene below them. When she finally looked back up, their eyes met.

"I'm glad this assignment today turned out to not be just another training exercise. This was much more fun." She looked a bit shy at that confession.

"Yeah. I'm glad, too. This was much better."

Beau's first thought was how pretty she looked when she smiled, followed shortly by his second thought, that he bet she would make a great mom. *Shit* comprised the whole of his third thought.

Why the hell was he thinking crap like that about her? They couldn't be together like that. They could work together like this. That was all. Perhaps, if he could control himself and if she agreed, they could start to run together again without Crash to chaperone, but that was all they could have. They could never, ever sleep together.

And it wasn't just because of the damn fraternization rules that half of the troops on camp flaunted daily. Well, not totally because of the rules or the consequences for getting caught breaking them.

Getting caught and losing his position this far into his career would suck. But more, he couldn't have sex with her because Carrie wasn't the kind of girl you had sex with once and forgot. She deserved more than that from the man in her life. And for starters, Beau wasn't sure he was in any shape to give her more at this point in his life.

Sex on camp was a big no-no, but falling in love was an even bigger one, for him especially, with one failed marriage already in his past. And the way she occupied his mind constantly, day and night, he wasn't sure he wouldn't fall in love with her once he'd fully felt the joy that was Carrie.

He was still watching her face when he saw it change and knew immediately she'd heard something over the communications unit.

"What's up, Tech Sergeant?"

"There's an emergency on a ship stationed in the sea just to the north of us. The USS Montgomery. They need a medivac ASAP. We're already up in the air. We would be the quickest to respond."

Beau turned to address the pilot. "Do we have the fuel to get to the Montgomery?"

"Affirmative."

"Tech Sergeant, relay the coordinates to the pilot and tell base that we're good to go."

The emergency on the Montgomery turned out to be a kid who had cracked his skull real good on the rudder of an aircraft. Hard enough he definitely had a concussion and could possibly need surgery, dependant on the results of a CT scan for internal bleeding. The ship's surgeon didn't feel they had the facilities to handle it on board. The kid needed to get to the hospital in Djibouti where they were better equipped to deal with traumatic head injuries.

Beau's part in the rescue mission was simple. His crew had to pick up the sailor on the Montgomery, transport him to the hospital in Djibouti and drop him off before heading back to camp.

Watching Carrie kick into battle mode, or in this case rescue mode, made her even more attractive than before. She was good at the everyday stuff, but to watch the calm cool concentration on her face, the efficiency in her every action during an emergency... It was a big turn on.

By the time they'd landed and filed their reports, Beau could barely function for wanting her. When she left the meeting room, he followed.

Running to catch up with her, he called, "Carrie."

By now it was beginning to get dark. He caught up with her behind a water station, the side sheltered from view of any passers-by.

Carrie stopped and turned to face him. “Yeah?”

She’d hardly gotten the single word out when he grabbed both of her arms and slammed his mouth hard against hers. After barely a moment of surprised hesitation, she kissed him back, her mouth opening to his, enthusiastically welcoming his tongue with hers.

Beau dropped his hold on her arms in favor of tangling his hands in her hair, pulling the silky strands out of the bun so they tumbled down to touch the top of her shoulders. He groaned at the soft tantalizing feel of it against his skin, imagining what her hair would feel like against his naked, sweat-soaked body after he had tumbled her into his bed and made long, sweet love to her.

Her hands came up to grasp his head, like she wanted to make sure this time he wouldn’t pull away. She needn’t have worried. He couldn’t have stopped kissing her at that moment even if he wanted to.

She pressed closer, as if she couldn’t get enough of their bodies to touch. This close, there was no way she could miss his arousal, but at that point he didn’t care. He wanted her to feel what she did to him. What she had been doing to him for weeks.

He pulled away from her warm welcoming mouth just long and far enough to say, “This is how I wanted to kiss you the other night."

"Then why didn't you? Why did you run away?" Her voice sounded husky, from desire or hurt he couldn't tell.

"Because I want you so badly it scares the hell out of me."

The sound she made was half laugh, half sob. "Me, too."

"Oh, god. Carrie. What the hell are we gonna do?" It wasn't a question he expected an answer to since his mouth was immediately upon hers again.

As his hands roamed down her body, he wished they were wearing anything else besides the restrictive flight suits. And while he was wishing, he wished they were anywhere else besides here so he could strip her naked and take her the way he'd imagined so many times.

He never wanted this kiss to end but reality began to creep in. They were by no means somewhere private. Not even close. And he was not about to get caught and in trouble for just kissing. Making love to Carrie would be another story. His suspected being with her that way would be worth the risk to his career should they get caught.

Beau, thinking with his little head apparently, was even beginning to think that loving Tech Sergeant Carrie Armstrong would be worth a court marshal and possible dishonorable discharge. He realized that thought should alarm him, but it didn't, which in itself was a frightening concept.

He broke away again, noticing that each time he ended the kiss with her seemed more difficult than the last.

Beau glanced around them from their shelter behind the small hut in the fading light. "We can't do this here."

Carrie nodded. "I agree. So where then?"

Though frustrated he didn't have an answer for her, Beau couldn't help but grin at that question. If he had any doubt she was as willing as he, it was erased. That was it then, they were going to do this and damn the consequences.

Now, if only he could get his brain to function and come up with a time and a place they could be alone to consummate this relationship. If they were very careful and really smart about this, there was a good chance they'd get away with it.

"I don't know," he finally said. He was suddenly having a hell of a time thinking with her so close. He hated to admit it, but he could use Crash and his never-ending suggestions about now.

"What about tonight while everyone is drunk at the Cantina?" she suggested.

Beau smiled, remembering she barely drank and never went to Cantina, and shook his head. "It's only Wednesday.

It's never very crowded at the Cantina during the week. But you're on the right track. Saturday night there's this huge comedian from back home doing a show there. I mean *everybody* here will be at Cantina to see him. The rest of the camp will be as deserted as a ghost town."

Carrie nodded, her hands pressed against his chest now. He was certain she could feel his heart pounding through the canvas material. "Okay. Where should we meet? And then where should we go?"

Beau could swear she blushed in the dim light when talking about where they would go to do what they both wanted so badly.

"My tent?" he suggested. "Yours is out of the question. Not just because of Cindy, but women are too nosy in general. No offense but if any of my men see us, they will keep their mouths shut. We protect each other's backs."

She nodded. "No, you're right." Then she hesitated. "Okay. Saturday night then. Um, I guess we shouldn't be seen together between now and then so no one gets suspicious."

He knew she was right, but he couldn't face not seeing her. "No. Let's just keep acting normal. We'll run together, we'll eat together when we're both at chow at the same time, I'll keep requesting you as my SatCom operator, just like we've been doing. It will look more normal if we don't change our habits."

His motives were purely selfish in his suggestion, which would insure they spent lots of time together each day, but she agreed with a quick nod. And then he couldn't keep his hands off of her. Beau grabbed Carrie for one more, much too brief kiss.

Finally reluctantly pulling away, he said, "You better go before I can't stop myself and I find out exactly what you're wearing under that flight suit right here behind the water station."

Carrie grinned. "All right. I need to grab a shower before chow anyway."

The image of Carrie soapy and wet did nothing to reduce the pressure of his rock hard erection. Beau groaned and let his forehead drop to hers. "You had to put the picture of you in the shower in my head."

She laughed teasingly. It was the sexiest thing he'd ever heard. "Oh. I'm sorry, Beau. I really didn't mean to."

"It's alright." His hands cupped her face and he kissed her one last time, eventually pulling back and saying, "Okay, you *really* have to go now."

Carrie nodded and Beau felt grateful that she broke their physical contact by stepping out of his reach because he wasn't strong enough to do it himself. She turned to go, then paused to glance over her shoulder and say two words,

"Black lace."

"Excuse me?" Beau really hoped she hadn't meant what he thought she did.

"That's what's under my flight suit. Lace-edged, boy shorts style underwear. Black."

In agony, Beau swallowed hard at that image. "Ah, Jesus, Carrie."

He watched her laugh as she walked around the corner and out of sight. He waited a few seconds, then walked around the front of the water station where he reached inside, took out a big handful of ice and shoved it into the front of his flight suit, down deep into his own navy blue boxer briefs.

All he could think as the ice melted and wet his still raging hard-on, soaking the cotton of his underwear, was that it would be a long couple of days until Saturday night.

Chapter Ten

Beau glanced up nervously from his reclining position in his rack as Crash rapped his knuckles against the wooden doorframe of the cube. "You ready to head to Cantina? The show starts in an hour and we won't be able to get a coupla' seats together if we don't get over there right now."

Ready for his Oscar-winning performance, Beau put one hand on his stomach and grimaced. "I don't think I'm gonna make it, man."

"What? You've been talking about seeing this comedian dude since we heard he was coming to camp."

It was true. He had been, but between seeing some comedian, no matter how famous, or being with Carrie, there was no contest. But in hindsight, he'd wished he had kept his mouth shut about the comedian to begin with so Crash wouldn't be suspicious. A suspicious Crash was *not* a good thing.

Beau shook his head vigorously. "I know, Crash. But there's no way I'm gonna make it tonight."

"Why? What's wrong with you?"

Damn, since when had Crash turned into his mama, worrying about his health?

"It must a' been something I ate. I've got nasty shit coming out a' both ends." That image ought to end the inquisition. Beau thanked god he'd had the fish at dinner and Crash hadn't. The possible food poisoning insinuation was actually believable.

His supposed friend took one giant step back. "Eww. Too much information there, buddy. Okay. Well, if you feel better later, you know where I'll be."

Beau nodded. "I doubt I'm going anywhere but the head tonight, but thanks." And then he was alone again and counting the minutes until the time he'd told Carrie to meet him there.

He listened to the last few guys empty out of the tent and head noisily for the Cantina, one complaining to the other that they'd never get a seat this late. And then, it was blissfully quiet, until Carrie's soft knock sounded on the outside door.

Beau flew out of his rack and was to the door in seconds, flinging it open. With a quick glance into the darkness, he stepped back so she could enter. "Did anyone see you?"

"No. It was just like you said. There's not a soul out there. Everyone's at the Cantina."

She smiled hugely and his heart fluttered in his chest like he was some schoolboy and this was his first time. Although, it was their first time together, and that was important enough in itself.

"Is the coast clear here?" she continued softly, almost nervously.

Beau nodded and then swallowed hard, afraid to touch her until he asked this question. "You sure this is what you want?"

"Oh, yeah."

"If we get caught…"

She shook her head. "I'm okay with the risk. Are you?"

He nodded. "Hell yeah. But I want you to be fully aware of…"

She pressed one finger to his lips, causing them to tingle at her touch. "We've been really careful. Right?"

He nodded.

"Then we won't get caught so there's nothing to worry about. Which cube is yours?"

He hooked a thumb in the right direction. "Third one down."

She smiled mischievously and started a hip-swaying stride toward his cube as she pulled her tank top up and over her head, revealing a black bra hooked across her back. His mouth began to water as she kept walking.

With the tank top dangling from one wrist, she reached back behind her to grab the clasp in each hand but didn't unhook it quite yet. Pausing in his doorway, she glanced back. "Are you going to join me?"

Beau managed somehow to nod. "Oh, yeah," he said.

"Good." And then she unhooked the bra, giving him just a glimpse of the side of one creamy white breast before she disappeared into his cube and out of sight.

"God help me," he murmured to himself and followed her on feet that he couldn't have stopped even if he had wanted to.

By the time he reached the doorway, she was already naked and lying on top of his blanket. She was gorgeous, from the tips of tiny pink-tinged toenails to the tops of her blush-colored nipples. He hissed in a breath between his teeth. "Oh my god."

Carrie giggled. "Thank you, I think. Now, you are way overdressed."

Beau kicked off his flip flops and with shaking hands,

pulled off his own tank top and shorts, pausing momentarily at his boxer briefs. But fair was fair, and she was totally, gloriously, naked before him. Besides, the thin knit cotton wasn't hiding his raging hard-on anyway. He pulled off the last item and flung it onto the top of his footlocker where his other clothes had landed.

He noted with some satisfaction that Carrie's discarded things were there under his, just as Carrie herself was about to be under him.

Not knowing what part of her to indulge in first, Beau lay down on his side next to her in the narrow bunk. Dipping his head, he pulled the tip of one perfect nipple into his mouth and tasted the salt of her skin.

Carrie moaned softly as he let his right hand run leisurely up the length of her thigh until he glanced up at her and saw a look cross her face that stopped his hand in mid-motion.

"What's wrong?"

"I don't do this with everyone, Beau. I don't want to stop, I just want you to know that you, this, is special for me." The fear he thought otherwise shown clearly in her eyes, even in the dim light of his cube.

Relieved to be able to ease her mind, Beau shook his head. "Baby. I know you don't do this often, if ever. Neither do I. This is special to me, too, believe me." And then he laughed.

"What's so funny?"

"The day you arrived, the Airman who met your flight told me your nickname was Ice Queen."

Carrie frowned, marring her perfect forehead with wrinkles. "That's not very nice."

He regretted what he'd said immediately. In fact, why the hell were they talking at all? He finally had a naked Carrie in his bed, Beau could think of much better things they could be doing. But now she looked pissed and he had to come up with a way to fix it.

He brought his hand up to cup her face and shook his head. "Stop. It's not a bad thing. Trust me. I'd take you and your ice queen reputation over Cindy and *her* rep any day, and you know it. I couldn't get her skanky ass out of my bed fast enough."

Carrie scowled. "Don't remind me. I hope you washed the blankets."

Beau laughed. "Immediately. Now can we stop talking about other people who don't matter so I can kiss you? Because if I don't get to do that soon, I think I may die."

Finally, she smiled again and joked, "Wouldn't want that, would we?"

"Definitely not." Beau mirrored her smile until his lips touched hers, and then there was nothing humorous about how he felt. A sound he barely recognized as coming from inside of him rumbled from deep in his chest as he crawled half on top of her.

Her mouth opened beneath him, welcoming his tongue as it probed deeply inside her just like his cock ached to do lower.

He slid his left arm beneath her to press her warm body more closely to his as his right hand made its way to the apex of her thighs. When she spread her legs to give him access, he thought he might very well have a coronary, his heart pounded so hard. He felt the slick wetness waiting for him there and knew there was no way he would leave this earth before he'd taken her completely. He would make any deal with God or the Devil to have Carrie first.

Spreading her with one fingertip, he delved deeper, found her clit and teased it relentlessly until it was swollen and he knew, oh so sensitive. Carrie panted and shook beneath his touch, until her hips began to buck off the bed.

He kissed her harder as she came, her cries barely stifled by his hungry mouth. They should be quieter, but at the moment, Beau didn't care about "shoulds". He had wanted, too badly and for too long, to hear her as he drove her over the edge of pleasure. It was even better than he'd imagined.

Carrie's hand grasped at his as he continued to push her

further, until she finally succeeded in pulling his fingers away from her saying, "I want you inside me."

He couldn't agree more as he went to cover her with his body.

"Wait. Do you have a condom?" she asked breathlessly.

Good thing she remembered because his brain wasn't functioning at the moment.

Beau stifled the guilt as he reached beneath the pillow and pulled out one of the two condoms he'd stolen earlier from the long strip Crash had brought with him from home. He'd probably never notice the two missing from his footlocker since Beau had not known of him using any as yet.

Grabbing his erection in one hand, Carrie took the foil packet from him with the other and all thoughts of Crash and his sex life disappeared from Beau's mind. He was so far gone he probably couldn't have given her his name, rank, and serial number had she asked. What little blood remained in his brain rushed lower when she covered him.

Rolling on top of him now, Carrie straddled his hips, and he made no protest. Even though Beau didn't share his tiny cube, he still had bunk beds, like all the rest of the guys. Luckily, the top bunk left enough room for her to sit mostly upright as she gently guided him to her slick entrance.

Beau's stomach twisted and tightened at the beautiful sight of Carrie poised above him. And when she lowered herself over him, sheathing him slowly and completely as she closed her eyes and sighed, he felt his balls tighten, too, dangerously close to coming just from the feel of being inside of her.

He grit his teeth as she began to move above him, slowly, rising up and down, causing him the best kind of agony. The mingled scent that was uniquely Carrie surrounded him, a combination of citrus shampoo, minty lip balm, and aroused woman.

She dipped her head to his and nibbled on his earlobe. Beau closed his eyes against all of the incredible sensations assaulting him at once. He wanted this to last forever, or at least longer than sixty seconds, but the way he felt, he wasn't sure he could hold out much longer than that.

And when Carrie changed her pace as her breath began to quicken and he felt her muscles squeezing him inside of her, he really feared for his ability to hold on.

"Oh, god. Beau. I'm coming again."

He groaned his acceptance of the inevitable as he followed right behind her, pumping into Carrie hard and fierce as he came, too.

She collapsed her slight weight weakly on top of him, leaving his softening penis still nestled inside of her, right where he wanted to remain for a very long time. With that thought Beau realized, he could love this girl.

Hell, he was afraid he already did and falling in love was the dead last thing he ever thought would happen to him again in this lifetime, especially in Djibouti, of all places.

Not sure whether he was running from the truth, or toward it, Beau flipped Carrie over and began moving gently within her until he hardened again.

To the soft sound of Carrie's cries, Beau continued thrusting until he stopped thinking totally and just felt.

Chapter Eleven

"Hi." A seated Carrie smiled up at Beau and his heart skipped a beat.

Putting down his chow tray, he replied with a grin, "Hi, back."

There wasn't much they could say or do while in the crowded dining hall, but just being together was enough to make them both smile, and even blush, now days.

Although, being alone and in bed would have been even nicer for both of them.

That thought warmed Beau from head to toes and a few key areas in between. He glanced up from the tempting image and found Carrie pushing her food around on her plate without taking a bite.

"Something wrong? I mean, I know the meatloaf isn't exactly filet mignon, but it isn't that bad today," Beau joked.

She treated him to a small smile that didn't reach her eyes. "Did you hear about the detachment they're sending to Ethiopia?"

Beau nodded. He had heard about it. In fact, he'd been damned happy that his commander didn't want him to go. Luckily he was needed here in Djibouti, because a three-month long mission that would take him away from camp and Carrie was much, much too long. If he was sent to Ethiopia, chances were good that by the time he returned it would be time to go home to the States where he and Carrie would be stationed thousands of miles apart.

"I'm on the list of those up to go," she revealed, her face looking pained.

His fork, laden with ketchup-covered meatloaf, stopped halfway to his mouth as Beau asked, "You're going?"

"Well, I'm lying my ass off and doing a hell of a dance trying to come up with excuses why they should send one of the other guys and not me. I think I have a good chance of getting out of it since I'd be the only woman on the det. But, Beau, what if I can't get out of it and I have to go?"

He longed to reach out and touch her hand but couldn't, not here and now among all these eyes. Instead, he said,

"Carrie."

She focused on his face from across the table as she looked miserably at him. "Yeah?"

"If you have to go, then I'll get myself assigned to the det, too."

"You could do that?" For the first time during this discussion, she looked hopeful.

"I'll sure as hell try. Now let's not worry any more about it until there's something to worry about. You may not have to go at all, but if you do, we'll deal with it then. Okay?"

Carrie gave in with a halfhearted nod. "Okay."

The subject was dropped for the moment, but Beau couldn't help but think about it privately, planning and plotting about how to get himself assigned to go with her if it came down to that. Actually, it wouldn't be so bad being away from the prying eyes at camp, not if they were together, even in frigging Ethiopia.

When they had both finished their meal and he could procrastinate no longer Beau reluctantly left Carrie to go do her work and made his way back to this office, only to find Crash there, arms folded and obviously wanting to talk about something.

"Hey, Crash. What's up?"

"Folks are starting to talk."

"What else is new?" Beau shrugged, but his nonchalance on the outside didn't quite reach his insides because this time there was something to talk about. The slow sway of Crash's head got Beau's back up. "What?"

"You need to take this seriously."

Crash was giving him advice about being serious now? Him? The one Crash always teased for being too serious?

"There is nothing to take seriously." Beau swallowed hard, hoping Crash couldn't read the lie on his face.

"Yeah, there is. How many times have I caught you and your own personal SatCom operator whispering, or making eyes at each other across the chow table? You don't think it looks odd that she's the only one who ever goes up with you? And then there are the days I worked night shift and you two went running alone…"

"What about them?"

"You disappear for a little too long and come back sweaty all right, but not looking like you got that way from running."

Shit. Crash had noticed their runs had gotten longer. It figured they'd get caught when they weren't even doing anything. It's not that they hadn't considered a quickie out on the run trail, but there wasn't any privacy there so that idea had been quickly squashed. But they did take their time lately and draw their runs out longer than before, both reluctant to leave each other during one of their few moments a day alone together.

At least this particular accusation wasn't true, even if all the rest may well be. Beau shook his head, scowling, he hoped convincingly. "You're crazy."

Deny, deny, deny.

"I don't want to see you in trouble, or worse, kicked out of the Corps when you're what? Eight years away from retirement?"

"Six," Beau corrected and then laughed bitterly. "And this is pretty funny coming from you. Considering you were the one who told me to go out and get laid in the first place."

Crash's brow shot up to his hairline. "So you're saying I'm right, then. It's not just talk. You two are fucking."

That terminology and Crash's tone of voice brought Beau to his feet. "And maybe you should fucking shut up." He emphasized each word with the stabbing poke of his index finger into Crash's broad chest. The man in front of him may be bigger, but Beau was angrier.

"Ah, Jesus, Beau! It is true." A pained look crossed Crash's face, right before the light bulb above his head lit up and his eyes opened wide with realization. "You were with her that night you didn't come to Cantina, weren't you? Comedy night. You didn't come with me because you had plans with her! Food poisoning, my ass. I knew the only thing that would keep you away from no limit on the beer and seeing that comedian you love would be a piece of that hocake's sweet ass."

The last comment was too much for Beau and pushed him right over the edge of insanity.

Since he didn't make a move to defend himself, Beau assumed Crash never even saw the fist that connected soundly with his jaw, sending him reeling into the filing cabinet.

Beau's best friend, although probably not for much longer after that punch, righted himself and fingered his jaw with a look of astonishment on his face, but the shock had nothing to do with Beau's attack on him. "Holy fuck. You're in love with her!" Crash accused.

"What? No! Why the hell would you say that?" His own recent realization of that truth, and the fact that Crash had guessed it so easily, had Beau stuttering.

"It's written all over your face. Anybody could see it. And I've never seen you lose your cool like this before. Especially not over a chick. Jesus, Beau. We've disagreed before but hell, you've never punched me!" Crash scowled, still gently probing the red mark on his chin.

Beau sighed. "I'm sorry I hit you. I didn't mean it."

"Forget that. You punch like a girl, anyway. But

dammit, Beau. I told you to go out and get some pussy. I never told you to fall for the girl. There's a line between just fucking and fucking for keeps. You crossed that line and if it's this obvious to me, it sure as hell is to all the other eyes on camp that something is going on. Shit." Crash drawled the last word out, slow and long as only a true southerner, born and bred, could. "Now what the hell are you gonna do?"

"Nothing, 'cause none of it is true. There was no sex and I'm not in love with her so drop it."

Crash had looked as if all would be forgiven, including the swing he'd taken at him, if Beau just admitted it were all true. But Beau's refusal to do that was getting Crash angry. "Bullshit it ain't true." His friend's voice rose.

"I'm not discussing this any…"

The pointless conversation was interrupted by a loud knock and the sudden appearance of their OIC's less than happy-looking face poking through the door that swung open before either man could say, "Come in."

"Staff Sergeant Adams. I need to see you in my office. ASAP."

Beau didn't need to see the look on Crash's face to know what he was thinking. The OIC must have heard the rumors, too. The question was, how the hell did everyone seem to know about their one night together when he and

Carrie thought they had been so careful? Not that it mattered much now how they all knew because it was more than obvious, the jig was up.

"Yes, sir." On his way out the door, Beau said to Crash over his shoulder, "Talk to you later." He only hoped that *later* wouldn't be goodbye as he boarded a plane for home to be court marshaled.

Carrie walked toward Beau's office, dressed and ready for their run. He'd said he would meet her in the usual spot at the usual time, but when he didn't show, she figured he must have gotten tied up late at work.

She hoped he wouldn't have to miss their run. Since that night they were together, it seemed Carrie lived for the moments they had together. Even if it was just eating a meal or running on the trail, being with Beau was far preferable to being without him.

They hadn't been able to be alone again, physically, the way they had been last Saturday night, and that left Carrie full of longing for every one of the two long nights since then. But as much as she loved his body, she loved him, all of him, even more, and would take any time they could get together, even if it wasn't private time.

Love. She thought the word easily even though she

hadn't told him, and had no intention of doing so. But in her own head, when she thought of Beau, when she looked at him, or managed to touch him casually, that was the word that leapt to her mind.

When Carrie arrived at the office and looked around, all she found was Crash, working the night shift. "Hey there, Crash. Is Beau getting dressed for our run?"

Beau's best friend let out a bitter-sounding laugh. "Getting dressed down, more like."

She frowned. "What's up? Did something happen?"

Crash laughed again. "You tell me, sugar. Did something happen?"

Carrie's heart leaped into her throat. "Um, no. Not that I know of." *Liar, liar, pants-in-a-heap-next-to-the-bed on fire.*

"Sit down, Tech Sergeant Armstrong."

Where Crash was concerned, it seemed she'd gone from *Carrie,* to *sugar*, to the very formal and not so friendly *Tech Sergeant Armstrong* in a matter of seconds.

Carrie swallowed the lump in her throat and sat without speaking, afraid her voice wouldn't work anyway.

"Did Beau ever tell you about why he enlisted?"

What did this have to do with anything? "Yeah. He said some tough Gunny at a recruiting station in Georgia got him hooked with the pride of serving speech."

"That's only part of it, sweetheart."

Now she was *sweetheart.*

"His dad left them when he was pretty young. His mom struggled to support the four kids. You know he's the only boy, right? Just Beau with his mom and three sisters. He started working in the fields at fourteen years old to help put food on the table. Do you know what it's like to be a kid and have to grow up before your time? To not be able to go to the doctor when you're sick because you don't have health insurance? To worry where your next meal is coming from when other teenagers are out partying?"

He paused and waited until she shook her head and said so softly she wasn't sure he heard, "No."

"Didn't think so. Growing up like that does something to a guy. Some men would have turned to crime. I've seen it happen. Easier to rob a liquor store or deal drugs than work hard. Not Beau though. He got a real job as soon as he was legally old enough. Then he decided to make a career of the military knowing that if he did, his future would be secured and he'd never lack for anything the way he did as a child. He's just a few years away from retiring with full pension and lifetime benefits, if he makes it to retirement, that is. Right now, it's doubtful he will."

Carrie glanced up at Beau's friend and swallowed hard as bile began to work its way into the back of her throat.

"Why?"

"Because fraternization is an offense worthy of a dishonorable discharge. You've been in long enough to know that."

Carrie pulled strength she didn't know she possessed from somewhere deep inside her and looked Crash straight in the eye. "Yeah, I do know that."

He continued, "And yeah, we all know it happens and plenty of folks get away with it, but when you start flaunting it in public and spending every second of the day together, the higher ups can only turn a blind eye for so long. You know what I mean?"

Her eyes blurred with unshed tears as she nodded.

Carrie watched Crash's face soften a bit. "The shame is, people round here talk crap about things they know nothing about. They see a man and a woman spending time together around camp, makes them talk even if there's nothing there worth talking about. The bigger shame is that people get hurt by it. But I'm sure Beau will straighten things out with the OIC. He's been in 14 years. He knows how to take care of himself. But still, so close to retirement, it would be a real shame…"

The OIC? Carrie's eyes opened wide and she feared the answer to her question. "What happened with the OIC?"

"Beau got called in. Someone said they saw you

sneaking out of his tent just before closing time at the Cantina on comedy night."

Oh god. They had thought they had been so careful…

Crash went on. "The good thing is, it seems the accuser has a checkered history at this camp. So when Beau swore he was in his tent alone sick all night, and I backed him up that I'd spent the night at the Cantina drinking with you until closing time, the OIC was inclined to believe Beau. Then Zippy, who'd worked the bar that night, suddenly remembered seeing you there with me, after I reminded him of course. The bar was so busy that night it would have been easy for him to forget one girl. There still may be a report put in Beau's file regarding the allegation, but the OIC said he thought he could safely ignore the accusation this one time since it seemed unfounded."

Carrie breathed again for the first time in what seemed like forever. Crash had apparently worked fast and efficiently to get Beau's ironclad and totally bogus alibi set in motion. Thank god Carrie had spent the afternoon doing laps at the pool or her own OIC might have been able to find her to question her. She wouldn't have known to say she was at the Cantina with Crash. Damn, she could have screwed up everything and gotten them all in trouble for lying. That realization made her sick to her stomach.

Crash continued. "I would just hate to see another

accusation like this one surface again. More than one and the higher ups won't be able to dismiss it so easily. They might decide to investigate further. You know what I mean?"

Carrie knew exactly what Crash was saying. He had covered for them, but the affair couldn't continue. They couldn't keep risking all of their careers. Not with the busybodies she lived with at camp out to get them both. Even if they didn't get kicked out of the service, they could easily lose their ranks and have a black mark on their service records forever.

Burying deep the feelings that threatened to bring a torrent of tears to her eyes, she nodded. Crash looked satisfied with that.

The door to the office flung open and a breathless Beau, dressed in his usual shorts and tank top, flew in. "Hey! Here you are. I'm sorry I was so late. Something came up. You ready to run?"

Beau was trying so hard to act casual, Carrie wondered if he would tell her anything at all about the charges brought to him by his OIC, the ones that could have led to his dishonorable discharge…because of her. She shakily rose from her chair and Beau took that as her consent that she was ready to run. In reality, she was surprised she could stand. Her body felt numb.

"See you later, Crash," Beau called, holding the door open for her.

Crash sent Carrie a meaningful glance behind Beau's back and said flatly, "Later."

They had to be a mile into their run before Beau broached the subject. "So, I…uh…got called into the OIC's office this afternoon."

"Yeah?" It nearly killed her to not say more, to wait and let him tell her what he wanted to in his own time.

Beau paused for so long Carrie began to doubt he was going to say more, until finally, he continued, "Yeah. No big deal. Cindy's up to her old tricks again, spreading rumors about you and me. The lieutenant wanted me to be aware. Oh, and if anyone asks, I was sick in my tent and you were at the comedy show with Crash until closing. Just to be safe."

Carrie stopped and Beau had to put on the brakes and come back to where she'd halted.

"That's it? That's all?" she asked incredulously when he made so light of the very serious situation.

It was no surprise Cindy had been the one to make the accusation. It all made sense. Cindy was probably sneaking out of some guy's tent herself after her own drunken midnight booty call when she'd seen Carrie. Of all the people on camp to see them, Cindy was probably the one and only person who would report the indiscretion. The hypocrite.

Beau nodded casually. “That’s all. Everything’s fine. I just thought that you should know. We’ll have to be really careful from now on though.”

They had thought they had been careful!

When it was clear he wasn’t going to tell her anymore, she nodded, nearly stricken speechless. “Okay.”

Then she picked up their pace and ran until the pain of what she knew she would have to do was masked by the aches in her body.

Chapter Twelve

Carrie realized when you let someone into your heart, deep inside your soul, you opened yourself up to a hurt like no other. You basically handed them the power to wound you as surely as if you passed them a combat knife and asked them to use it to carve up your body.

She had opened her heart to Beau and invited him deeper inside than she had allowed anyone in her life, ever. And the thought of leaving him, even though it was her own choice, hurt as intensely as if he had flayed her open with her own regulation K-bar knife and let her guts spill out onto the dirt. But what other choice did she have?

None. That answer was more than obvious. And that was what sucked the most.

Beau nuzzled her neck, nibbling playfully as his breath brushed warm and moist against her skin, dragging her away from her thoughts. She closed her mind and memorized the sensation, willing the tears to stay inside and not spill out.

She and Beau were inside one of the helicopter hangers taking an incredibly stupid risk. She knew that. But when Beau had set up the rendezvous, saying he couldn't go another day without getting his hands on her, she had agreed. Carrie had agreed knowing, even though Beau did not, that it would be their last time together.

"God, Carrie. I want you so much. All the time. Just seeing you at chow, or at the comm unit up in the bird..." He grabbed her face with both hands and kissed her mouth hungrily.

She moaned softly as the pain and sadness ripped through her heart.

It was dark in the hanger, a night that no maintenance was scheduled. Only a dim yellow-tinted security light illuminated their hiding place. Both Crash and Zippy, who were already privy to their affair, hung outside within sight of but not too nearby the hanger's entrance. Carrie smothered the embarrassment that Beau had actually asked his crew to stand guard so she and he could have sex.

Beau had said he'd told them he and she only wanted to

be alone to talk, but Crash and Zippy weren't stupid, they knew the truth. The look Crash had shot her that evening at chow clearly spoke his disapproval at the idea, even though he agreed to help them. It didn't matter. She knew that this would be the last time they would have to impose on Crash and Zippy so she and Beau could be together. Ever.

That thought sent one tear cascading over the rim of her eyelid. She quickly reached up and brushed it away, grateful he wouldn't see it in the darkness as his mouth moved down her neck, working its way toward one of her t-shirt covered breasts.

He raised the hem of her shirt and unbuttoned her pants, slipping one hand inside her panties as he said softly, "I'd give anything for a bed right now. I want to make love to you properly."

The one thing Carrie didn't think she could handle at that moment was Beau being sweet and romantic. She didn't want gentle, it was going to make her cry and she knew once she started crying in earnest, she would never be able to stop.

She could not take him being tender and loving, not tonight, so Carrie spun to face the wall of the hanger, pushed her cammies and panties down to her ankles and spread her legs as far as she could while hampered by clothing. "Now, Beau. Please. Hard and fast," she whispered with her head turned just enough so he could hear from behind her.

She heard him laugh softly. "I like how you think, baby."

Anchored by his hands on her hips, Beau plunged into her. While Carrie braced her forehead and both hands against the wall of the hanger, Beau moved roughly behind her but it was still all she could do to hold back the tears as he loved her. He filled her perfectly, hitting her sweet spot with each stroke, driving her closer, and when he reached around and brought her to orgasm with his hand on her clit, she couldn't help it anymore and let the tears flow.

Beau shuddered behind her, burying his face in her hair to stifle his groan as he, too, came.

Breathing hard against her, Beau laid his warm cheek on her tear soaked one and then stilled. "Baby? Are you crying?"

She nodded. "I'm sorry. I'm okay. Really."

He pulled out of her and adjusted his pants before turning her toward him. Stepping back just far enough for her to reach down and retrieve her own pants, he took her in his arms as soon as she'd buttoned the top button and secured the belt.

"Carrie. Tell me. What's wrong, darlin'?"

She whispered her answer, "I just wish we could be

together."

Beau pressed his forehead against hers. "I know, baby. Me, too. I hate having to sneak around. We'll just have to do the best we can for now. Okay?"

She clamped down on the sob that threatened to erupt and nodded.

Letting out a big sigh, Beau said the unavoidable words she dreaded. "I hate to say this, especially with you upset, but I have to get going."

The plan was for him to leave the hanger first, meet up with Crash, and the two of them would go get a beer at the Cantina, making sure they were seen together. Meanwhile, Zippy would make sure the coast was clear, then come in and get Carrie, taking her to the chow hall for a late snack where they, too, would make sure they were seen together.

All these intricate plans, all these careers in jeopardy, and all Carrie could think of was that for once, she would rather be the one getting the beer instead of the snack. Facing leaving Beau forever, she could sure use the alcohol to numb her mind.

She did her best to hide her agony and forced out a soft response to Beau. "It's okay. You can go. I'm fine."

His mouth was on hers again, kissing her and then pulling away. "Mmmm. If I don't get out of here now, I'm not going to be able to leave. But cheer up. I'll see you in the morning for chow."

Beau brushed a hand over her damp cheek. She nodded, knowing it was not going to happen.

"Bye for now," he whispered with a smile in his voice.

Simply glad she somehow controlled her rising sob, Carrie knew she could not answer with a smile or the 'for now'.

"Goodbye, Beau."

Miserably, she bit her lower lip until she tasted blood as she watched him go.

Once alone in the hanger, Carrie waited impatiently for Zippy. She had to get this sham over with as soon as possible and get back to her tent. She had a letter to write, a bag to pack, and a transport to Ethiopia to catch at o-three-hundred hours. After that, there would be plenty of time to wallow.

"I don't know where Carrie was this morning. Maybe she's sick. You think I should go check on her?" Beau pulled the chair out from his desk and pushed the button that would boot up his office computer.

Crash frowned at him as if he'd lost his mind. "No, I don't! You can't go checking on her at her tent right under Cindy's nose. Are you crazy? You took an incredible risk last night as it is. Don't push it."

"What's up your ass? We didn't get caught so relax." Beau leaned back in his seat and waited for his computer to come to life as he thought about last night with Carrie.

Taking her up against the wall of the hanger hadn't been what he had in mind, although given where they were, their options were kind of limited. Either way, the sneaking around, the knowing Crash and Zippy were outside, having to keep their voices down so they didn't get caught, it had all been really hot. Just thinking about it made Beau want to find a way to repeat it and soon. He'd never thought of himself as being into risky sex, but judging from last night, he may well be.

Crash blew out a breath of air filled with frustration. "Well, don't expect me to cover for you again. If you want to risk your career for some pussy, that's fine, but I'm not risking mine."

Assuming Crash was just jealous that he wasn't the one getting any, which was the reason for the foul mood, Beau responded with a bored, "Yeah, whatever."

That elicited a disgusted huff from Crash as he flung his large frame into his own chair with a scowl while Beau, still flying high with sex hormones, smiled.

Then a white envelope with his first name written on it caught his eye. Frowning, he snatched it off the desktop and tore the sealed flap open. Taking out a single handwritten piece of notepaper, Beau read the signature first. *Carrie*. His eyes flew up to the first line.

Beau,

It turns out I couldn't get out of the Ethiopia det after all. I'll be gone by the time you get this. Sorry I didn't get to tell you in person.

It's been fun.

Carrie

The Carrie he knew and loved would never say goodbye for three months in a note. If she found out last minute late last night that she had to go, why the hell didn't she come knock on his tent door and tell him? Although, maybe she had been afraid she'd be seen. But still, they were friends and co-workers, it wouldn't look odd if she informed him she was leaving camp for three damn months!

The ending of the note sounded off, too. *It's been fun?* What the hell? Was she crazy? This was not his Carrie, the same woman who had cried when they made love last night. But there it was, written in her slanting script in black and white. Beau wanted to vomit from holding in his hand the physical proof that the woman he loved had left him so callously.

His face must have shown his shock, because Crash asked from across the room, "Beau? You okay? What's up?"

Answering seemed beyond his capabilities, so when Crash suddenly appeared next to his desk, Beau shoved the note at him and then silently left the office. Where he could go that his pain and anger wouldn't follow, he didn't know. All he knew was that he couldn't just sit there.

Chapter Thirteen

"Staff Sergeant Adams."

Beau welcomed the interruption as he looked up from the growing stack of paperwork on his desk to respond to the officer in charge. "Yes, sir."

Lieutenant Li closed the office door behind him and plopped down into the chair opposite Beau's. "There's a new SatCom operator on base. Just transferred in. I want you to show this Airman the ropes during the training tomorrow afternoon."

"Good to go, sir." Beau nodded and hid that, even six months after the fact, his chest still felt like someone was squeezing it at the mere mention of the words *SatCom operator*.

It didn't matter that Beau's butt was firmly planted in his desk chair at Marine Corps Air Station, New River, North Carolina, because his mind was back in Africa, filled with memories of *his* SatCom operator and how she had ripped out his heart.

How the hell long would it take for that wound to heal? And why the hell was his OIC still lounging there, forcing Beau to keep his features neutral?

Beau stared sightlessly down at the report on the top of the paperwork pile as he resisted the urge to bury his face in his hands in an attempt to scrub away the memories… The sound of Carrie's softly drawling voice, the feel of her firm muscles and long lean limbs beneath his hands, the way sinking himself deeply into her had made him lose all awareness of everything except for her and her soft cries as she came.

Damn it, his body still reacted to thoughts of her. But Carrie was gone. She'd left him and never looked back.

He'd emailed her, more than once right after she'd left, but she hadn't responded. Eventually his pain and his pride made him stop bothering. He knew that the others in the det to Ethiopia could access their email so it was obvious, Carrie simply didn't want to hear from him.

By the time the detachment returned, his time at Camp Lemonier had come down to a harried ending of packing up and transferring duties to his replacement. He didn't have time to seek her out during those last few days at camp and she sure as hell didn't try to find him.

He had to remember that. And the sooner he could get himself to remember *that* rather than all the rest, the better.

A light quick knock on the door thankfully yanked his traitorous mind back to the present.

"I got it," Li, with apparently nothing better to do, said as he rose from the chair.

Fine. If his lieutenant wanted to sit around in Beau's office and play doorman all day, who was he to question? Maybe if Beau somehow could accidentally "lose" all the extra chairs in the office, visitors would be less likely to dawdle. It was definitely something to consider. Lately, he was really not into socializing, unless it took place at a bar and involved some mind-numbing whisky.

With a stifled sigh, Beau glanced at the door his OIC had opened, listening to him welcome whoever stood there just out of his sightline.

Then he heard her voice…

It didn't matter that he still couldn't see her, Beau was certain. The person standing just outside his door, the new Airman he was supposed to take up for the training, was Carrie.

Throat constricted, heart pounding, Beau forced himself

to not leap from his own chair, push his OIC aside and grab her. Although whether he wanted to kiss her silly or shake some sense into her, he couldn't decide. What he knew for a fact he wanted from the woman who had danced on his heart were answers. Only one answer, really. *Why?*

"Staff Sergeant Adams. This is Tech Sergeant Armstrong, the new SatCom operator I was telling you about." Li finished the introduction and now Beau had to find his voice or look like an idiot. What should he do? Pretend to not know her?

Carrie made the decision for them both. "Staff Sergeant. Nice to see you again."

Beau nodded formally. "Tech Sergeant Armstrong. You, too." *Yeah, right.*

"You two know each other?"

"Yes, sir. We worked together at Camp Lemonier a few months back," Carrie explained.

They'd done a hell of a lot more than *work* together, but from Carrie's cool tone, you'd never guess that.

"Good. Then the training should be a no-brainer. I'll see you both later." And with a nod, Li was gone, just when Beau was wishing he would stay.

"Beau..."

He had a moment of satisfaction when both her voice and her passive expression broke as she said his name.

Folding his arms, Beau leaned back in his chair, just as Crash walked into the office.

His friend, the only one on this earth who knew all of the sordid details besides the two of them, looked from Carrie, to Beau, and then back again. "Ah, shit," Crash muttered under his breath.

Who said Crash wasn't perceptive? Beau couldn't have said it better himself.

Carrie broke the silence first. "Hey, Crash."

Beau's friend shot him another concerned glance before saying, "Hey, Carrie."

Heart in his throat, Beau swallowed and said, "Crash."

"Yeah, Beau?"

"Can you give us a minute?"

"Yeah, sure. Take all the time you need." Crash couldn't have left the office faster if his ass had been on fire, but that didn't matter, because Carrie apparently had no intention of staying.

"I'm sorry. I tried to get reassigned the minute I found out they were sending me to New River but I couldn't. I'll manage it though. I promise. But until then, I guess I'll have to see you at the training. I'm sorry, Beau."

He thought he heard her sob as she turned and disappeared out of the door. He stood, but for the life of him, he couldn't bring himself to follow her. He was just still too damn hurt. Besides, what would he be chasing after? There was obviously nothing between them as far as she was concerned.

Beau was still standing there next to his desk when Crash came back into the office. “So what did she have to say?”

Beau shrugged. “That she was sorry she couldn’t get out of being transferred here.” He shook his head bitterly and wished for a beer to suddenly appear.

Crash cleared his throat and then said, “Beau, Carrie…”

“I don’t want to talk about her, Crash,” he warned with a growl.

“She left Djibouti to protect your career.”

Beau frowned. “How the hell do you know that?”

“The day you got called into the OIC’s office because of Cindy’s accusation, Carrie came looking for you.”

Beau remembered. He’d found her there with Crash, white-faced and silent.

“Go on.”

“I told her how your night together nearly got you in trouble. How you were risking getting thrown out of the Corps but more than that, I told her how important your career is to you because of your past. I really drilled it into her just how close you came to ruining your future that day because of her.”

"Ah, dammit, Crash. Why couldn't you just stay the hell out of my business?"

"Come on, Beau. You know I was right. You were thinking with the little head at the time."

"It was my problem, not yours."

"It sure as hell was my problem when you started dragging me and Zippy into it."

"I never asked you to be my alibi. You came up with that all on your own."

"To save your ass because I'm your friend." Crash shook his head. "And you're welcome."

Beau took in a deep, steadying breath as he decided what to do. He'd spent the last six months trying to hate Carrie for what she'd done and meanwhile, she'd done it to save him. This required a whole new set of feelings, guilt being at the top of the list.

"Look, Beau. Us fighting won't help shit. Go after her. We're Stateside now. If you lie low, you two could probably get away with shacking up together out in town and no one would be the wiser. You two can finally be together."

When Beau remained silent, Crash asked, "You do still want to be with her, don't you?"

A lot of time had passed but the fact he still couldn't get her out of his mind, even when he thought she'd callously dumped him told him the answer. He still wanted her. He still loved her. "Hell, yeah. I still want to be with her."

"Then go after her, Beau. What the hell are you waiting for?"

Beau didn't know himself, but whatever the reason, he was done standing around doing nothing. It was time he took action.

"I will!" Beau flung the door open and flew down the hall and out into the parking lot. He spotted Carrie getting into her car and sprinted to catch her.

Flinging open the passenger side door, he planted himself firmly in the seat and slammed the door.

"Beau?"

"Drive, Carrie."

"Why?"

"Because we need to talk and I don't want to do it here."

She sighed with reluctant resignation. "Where?"

"Just drive. I'll tell you where to turn."

Beau gave her directions to the Marina on base, instructing her to park and then to get out of the car. The site was beautiful, right on the water, but its charm was lost on him. All he could see was her.

Beau had camped at the Marina once with his squadron, so he knew his way around a bit. There was a private path into the woods. He grabbed Carrie's hand and led her there now.

"Beau, I'm not sure we..."

In light of her protest, he stopped and turned, deciding to get the discussion started before she bolted. Facing her with both hands on her arms to make sure she stayed put, Beau said, "Tell me exactly why you left."

She lowered her eyes, no longer able to meet his. "I told you in the note. I couldn't get out of the det."

He blocked out the pain of that note, knowing now after his talk with Crash that she had meant to wound him so he wouldn't try to contact her. "You mean you stopped trying to get out of it and instead asked to go, didn't you?"

Carrie frowned but didn't answer. "Beau, we almost got caught in Djibouti. Hell, we did get caught. Only your friends lying saved your career, both of our careers. There was no way we could have gone on the way we were with Cindy out to get us, watching every move we made and reporting it. Eventually our commanding officers wouldn't have been able to ignore what was going on. I made the right decision for both of us so just let it go. Please. Just let me go."

He knew she meant let her go out of his life, not just out of his grasp. But that was one thing he couldn't do.

"I know you left camp to save my career, but that was

not your choice to make." His grip on her arm lightened, but there was no way he was letting her go. Not now, not ever again. "Cindy isn't here. You and I are and I still want you."

A small sob escaped her as she turned her head so he couldn't see her face.

Beau pulled her into his arms and felt her start to shake. "Oh, baby. Why didn't you come to me first? We could have worked something out. I would have moved heaven and earth to be with you."

He felt her let out a short snort of a laugh. "That's exactly why I didn't come to you. You would have risked it all and I couldn't let you do that. It had to end. I had to end it."

Yeah, and he remembered how heartlessly she'd done it, too. The months of pain and anger he'd felt began to surface. Beau pulled back and looked down at Carrie's wet, tear-streaked face. "Dammit, Carrie. You couldn't have made things any worse if you tried. That 'it's been fun' note put me through hell."

"You? I was in hell, too, you know," she said defensively.

He sighed. "Yeah. I know. All this pain for both of us for nothing, Carrie, when you could have just come to me."

Finally she looked more angry than hurt. "Aren't you listening? I did it for you, you idiot, because I loved you," she whispered.

Well, that revelation was certainly not what he had been expecting. He stood there speechless for what felt like an eternity.

Finally, she shook her head. “It doesn’t matter now. I gotta go.”

“Oh, no, you don’t!”

Maybe he was still wounded and mad and definitely not prepared to confess his undying love to her—that was not something he would ever do lightly—but Beau refused to let her walk out on him again.

The kiss should have begun gently and tenderly given Carrie’s tearful confession, but somehow it turned wild, desperate, and crazed. They ended up against the base of a tree, hidden by leaves and bushes, pawing at each other’s clothes. It was risky, yes, but it seemed he lost all control of his reasoning abilities when he kissed her. And when she roughly grasped his erection through his uniform pants, all hope was lost.

In a struggle for dominance, Carrie freed him from both his cammies and his boxer briefs before she dropped down onto her knees on the ground and took him in her mouth. With a nearly Neanderthal growl, Beau realized he wouldn’t have cared then if the base MPs had pulled right up and demanded they stop at gunpoint.

She lapped at the tip of him, catching a drop of pre-come on her tongue. He groaned as she thrust him deep to the back of her throat and his knees felt weak. And when she stroked him with both her mouth and her hand, he lost all control, shooting hot spurts into the back of her throat as he grasped her head in his hands. At that point, he couldn't have stopped coming even if he'd had the mind to try.

Dropping down on his knees to be even with her, he grabbed her around the waist and they collapsed together against a fallen tree.

Carrie seemed to have the ability to cast a spell over him. Not only did he want her constantly, even after just having her, but his cock rose to the occasion effortlessly and repeatedly. That had been proven during the blissful few hours they'd spent in his bunk back in Djibouti. It was proving true again now in spite of the less than ideal location.

Not only did he want her again for selfish reasons, but Carrie still had yet to come. The one thing even better than taking pleasure himself was watching her as she did.

The way she was crazed as she stroked his cock until it was at full tilt again had him wondering, hoping really, that she hadn't had sex since they'd been together in Djibouti. Though he didn't have the nerve to ask, the thought that she hadn't been with another man since him made him extremely happy.

He hadn't been with anyone else, either. On one of his darker days, Beau had thought about going out to pick up a woman, any woman, to fill the gap Carrie had ripped in his life even if it was for just one night, but when it came down to it, he knew no one could replace her.

Damn, he wanted this woman for so many reasons.

He undid the buttons of her uniform pants and slid a hand inside as she kissed him wildly. Beau groaned when he found her wet and ready. As she pushed her pants down to her ankles, leaving them tangled around her boots, reality hit him hard. "Dammit. I don't have a condom, Carrie."

Eyes narrowed with desire, she said, "I don't care. Just make love to me."

She turned her back to him and he simply stared at the beauty of her thong-clad ass right there before him. Sliding the panties to the side while Carrie braced herself against an old, downed tree, Beau sunk himself deeply into her and felt her wet heat surround his unsheathed erection for the first time.

As his fingers found her sweet spot in front, Beau moved slowly and deeply within her from behind until he felt her grip him as she cried out. Only then did he speed his pace until he felt the familiar tingle inside him. With intense mingled pleasure and regret, he pulled out and shot his own release all over the ground.

Still breathing heavily, he collapsed onto the log and pulled Carrie toward him so she could lay her head on his chest.

Beau stroked her soft hair gently, picking out a piece of leaf as she leaned against him. He laughed. "Maybe one day we will be together in an actual bed, a nice big one."

Although, he would take her any way he could get her.

She whispered, "Nothing has changed, Beau. This is impossible."

"What do you mean?"

"We are impossible. How can we be together? We're both career military. We're here together in New River now, but three months from now one or both of us could be shipped off and stationed anywhere they want to send us. I could end up back in Germany and you could be in Hawaii again for all we know."

"Don't worry until there's something to worry about, Carrie."

She shook her head. "I can't live like that, Beau. I can't wait around for the rug to be yanked out from under me. I just can't. This was crazy what we just did and it can't happen again."

He was in such shock that she was willing to throw it all away and not even give them a try that he didn't protest when she rose and righted her clothes. He didn't even stop her as she turned and left him sitting there alone. When he heard her car start and peel out of the parking lot, the long walk from the Marina back to his building was the least of his worries.

When Beau finally arrived back at his office it was to find Crash waiting for him and the news he gave him did not improve his mood any.

"Li just stopped by to pass the word. Tomorrow's training is canceled," Crash informed him with an interested glance at his sweaty face.

"Ah, shit." Beau flung himself into his chair and grabbed the bottle of water on his desk.

Carrie had succeeded in leaving him for the second time in six months for the sake of his career, he'd had to walk a hell of a long way in the North Carolina heat, and now his one chance to be near her again was cancelled. Could this day get any worse?

Beau decided to get all of the unpleasantness out of the way. "Go ahead. Ask what happened with Carrie. I know you want to."

"Nope, I don't think I need to."

"Why not?"

"Because I talked to the new SatCom operator."

Beau frowned. "You mean Carrie?"

Crash shook his head, "No, man. I mean her coworker, the Airman who just called to introduce himself to you since he'll be replacing her."

"Replacing her?"

"Yup, because she's leaving for home on a month's leave."

Damn, that walk must have taken him longer than he thought. Long enough for his last hope to be washed right down the toilet.

Carrie arrived at the airport in Mississippi and immediately felt the familiar oppressively hot air that said home.

She glanced around, sure that her mother had said the family would be here to meet her at the airport. She realized it had been far too long since her last visit home. On one hand, that had worked in her favor. She hadn't taken a leave in over a year so when she asked, they didn't dare deny her last minute request. They'd approved her on the spot and immediately replaced her with another Airman.

On the other hand, the guilt that she'd let so much time pass between visits overwhelmed her, but compared to the pain of leaving Beau for the second time, it was nothing.

But surely her parents wouldn't leave her standing at

the airport…

"Need a ride?"

Carrie jumped as the deep achingly familiar voice startled her.

"Alan? Oh my god." She leapt into his arms and before she knew it, the sorrow and loneliness of the past few months caught up with her.

Alan pulled back and took her face in his hands as she tried to not sob too loudly. "Carrie Ann. What's wrong, baby girl? Surely I didn't get so ugly I make you cry."

She wiped at her face, embarrassed. "I'm sorry."

With a smirk, the Alan of her youth was before her as if no time had passed at all. And just like when they were kids, he tried to make her laugh as she cried by teasing her. Hands on his hips, he put on his best mean face and said deeply, "You better be sorry, woman! Now get in that car. Your mama sent me to get you. She's got supper waiting on you."

"Don't you ever talk to her like that again."

Carrie turned to find Beau, jaw set and fists clenched directly behind her.

"Beau? What…?"

"I think you should come with me," Beau said as he grabbed her arm and pulled her further away from Alan.

"Like hell she will!" Alan grabbed her other arm and

pulled her back closer to him and away from Beau.

"Get your fucking hands off of her," Beau grit out.

"Like hell I will. You let go of her," Alan countered.

Beau dropped his hold on Carrie, but to her horror, it was only so he could swing at Alan, catching the taller man in the chin hard enough to knock him back a step.

"What the hell?" Alan dropped his hold on her also. "Who the hell do you think you are?"

"I'm the man who's in love with her. Who the hell are you?"

Alan raised a brow and glanced at Carrie, who seemed incapable of doing anything besides remain speechless after Beau's unexpected confession of love.

"I'm her best friend," Alan informed him, "and if you really are in love with her, why the hell haven't I ever heard about you?"

Carrie swallowed and found her voice. "Alan, this is Beau. Beau, Alan."

Beau frowned. "Alan? The guy who beat you in that race in high school?"

Alan scowled in her direction. "Well, at least he knows who I am. Carrie Ann, would you like to let me know who he is and why he felt the need to punch me?"

"Alan, can Beau and I have a minute alone, please?"

His gaze traveled between the two of them before Alan

finally agreed. "A'ight, but I'm gonna be right over there where I can see you."

Carrie nearly laughed that Alan was trying to protect her from Beau. "Okay."

After Alan left, she could turn her full attention to Beau. "What are you doing here? How did you find me?"

He stepped forward and ran both of his hands up her arms. "Shh. I'll explain it all soon. But first, I need to ask you something. Back at the Marina. You said you left for Ethiopia because you loved me."

She nodded but didn't move, suddenly unsure of what he would say and unable to meet his eyes.

"I need you to tell me one more thing. You said you 'loved' me. Past tense?" he asked, looking almost afraid of her answer.

Now she did look up at him, directly in the eyes, as her face softened. "No." She sighed deeply. "Present tense. I still love you, Beau, maybe more than before."

She saw Beau's eyes drop to her mouth as she bit her lip, waiting for his answer. He ran his hand up and down her arm. "It's definitely present tense for me, too. I love you, Carrie."

Carrie smiled tearfully and took a deep shaky breath. "But nothing has changed, Beau. We're still in the same position we were in before. We still have the same problems standing between us."

Beau took a step closer to her. "I've figured that all out."

When she glanced up at him in surprise, he laughed and shrugged. "It was a long flight from North Carolina to here."

Carrie swallowed hard, afraid to hope. "So what do we do?"

She felt his thumbs nervously making small circles against her arms. "We get married."

"We what?"

"Marry me, Carrie. And not just because the military can't station us apart after we do, but because I love you and I don't want to live without you. The past six months have been hell and I never want to feel like that again."

When she didn't answer he squeezed her arms gently. "Carrie. Please answer me."

Smiling and crying at the same time, Carrie managed to nod. "Yes. I'll marry you."

Beau smiled and that was all the invitation she needed to crash against him.

Stroking her hair, he asked, "So, do you think your best friend is going to congratulate me or punch me back when we tell him?"

She laughed. "I'm pretty sure he'll be happy because

I'm happy."

"Are you happy, Carrie?"

She kissed him hard to show him before she pulled away and told him. "Very."

Beau continued, stroking her face while saying, "We are gonna make up for all that time we lost together. And from now on we talk about things and you are gonna promise me you will never do something as crazy as leaving me again the way you did in Djibouti."

Against his chest, Carrie said in a muffled voice, "I'm so sorry, Beau. I really am."

He laughed, sounding relieved to have her in his arms again. She understood completely, she felt almost weak over it herself.

"Don't worry. I'll come up with a few ideas of how you can make it up to me," he joked, eyebrows waggling suggestively.

Carrie pulled back to look up at him accusingly. "Are you being dirty at a romantic time like this?"

He looked a bit guilty when he said, "Um. Maybe just a little. Is that alright?"

"Yeah. It's alright," she laughed and when he smiled back at her, she felt her heart tighten.

Beau gave a very pointed, meaningful look at a nearby building. "You could start making it up to me right now…"

Carrie's eyes opened wide. "Beau! And before you ask, yeah, I think Alan will probably punch you out if you start taking off my clothes here and now!"

Beau laughed. It was a nice sound. After months of them both being miserable without each other, it was nice to see him happy.

"Kidding," he said.

"Oh, really? After the Marina, I'm not so sure."

Beau laughed and pulled her closer to cover her mouth in a kiss. Pulling away, Beau said, "God, Carrie. I am so in love with you."

Her heart pounded faster at those sweet words. "I love you, too. So much. I'll never willingly leave you again. I swear, Beau. You won't be able to get rid of me, even if you wanted to."

Beau had just one word to say to her in response. "Good."

"Good," she echoed and then noticed Alan getting antsy as he stood off to the side, trying not to watch her kissing Beau far too passionately considering her childhood friend was there. Which reminded her… "I hope you're ready to meet my parents."

"My new in-laws?" Beau pursed his lips and looked as if he was considering for a moment before he smiled broadly. "Never been readier, darlin'."

About the Author:

It all started in first grade when Cat Johnson won the essay contest at Hawthorne Elementary School and got to ride in the Chief of Police's car in the Memorial Day Parade...and the rest, as they say, is history. As an adult, Cat generally tries to stay out of police cars and is thrilled to be writing for a living. She has been published under a different name in the Young Adult genre, but Linden Bay is the first to release her romances.

On a personal note, Cat has one horse, too many cats, one dog, parakeets, fish, and a husband, and is not sure which of those gives her the most grief. Needless to say, she is very busy most days on her little 18th century farm in New York State. She plays the harp professionally and stresses that this does not mean she plays well. A past bartender, marketing manager, and Junior League president, Cat's life is quite the dichotomy, and on any given day she is just as likely to be in formal eveningwear as in mucking clothes covered in manure. Cat hates the telephone but loves email, and is looking forward to hearing from you.

Other works by Cat Johnson:

Trilogy No. 102: Opposites Attract

...a three-part lighthearted romp through the intertwining lives of six people who learn that in spite of everything you have to remember to live, love and laugh to be happy.

Taking a Leap: Bradley Morgan is the quintessential computer geek and nice guy, through and through. The only problem is that in his opinion, nice guys almost always finish last when it comes to hot women like his sexy co-worker Alyssa Jones. But things change after Alyssa finds her boyfriend cheating. Suddenly, nice guys like Brad don't look so bad. So when Brad agrees to ghostwrite the sex scenes for a romance novel as a favor for desperate client Maria White and asks for Alyssa's help after hours, she agrees wholeheartedly and things really start to heat up. Brad and Alyssa learn you should never judge a book by its cover, and that sometimes love requires a leap of faith.

Light my Fire: Amy Gerald's life is filled with whirlwind romance. Unfortunately, it's all on the pages of the romance novels she publishes. That is until she volunteers to cat-sit for her author friend Maria and meets Troy O'Donnell, the hunky fireman who lives next door. The problem is, this commitment-phobic consummate bachelor is far more willing to run into a burning building than allow love into his life. Troy will grasp at any excuse, even the ridiculous assumption that Amy is a lesbian, just to avoid his growing feelings for her. Amid a comedy of errors and misunderstandings, which includes Troy's first hilarious visit to a gay bar, Amy manages to light Troy's fire, but can she also conquer his fears?

Second Time Around: Antonio Sanchez thought that at 32 his life was all mapped out—wife, kids, career—until some major bumps in the road radically alter his course and send him careening right into the path of newly divorced Maddie Morgan. Suddenly thrust back into single life, Antonio moves back in with his old-fashioned parents and has to learn to juggle his kids, his job at the firehouse, and his role as Best Man for his newly engaged best friend Troy, all in addition to facing his unquenchable desire for Maddie. Throw in a slew of matchmaking friends and relatives, led by Maria whose apartment appears to be the Bermuda Triangle for lost lovers, and Antonio and Maddie discover just how complicated things can get. Can the pair prove that love really is better the second time around?

Trilogy No. 103: Red Hot & Blue

Trey: Special operative Trey Williams doesn't want a girlfriend, nor does he need one in his life. A distracted soldier is a dead soldier, that's his motto. The problem is, the woman who has been recruited to pose as his wife on a special assignment is proving to be more of a distraction than Trey can handle. What's a soldier to do?

Jack: Ordered by his superiors to take time off for his "mental health", Jack Gordon heads back to his hometown for two weeks of R&R. But then he meets Nicki Camp, the new hand his brother has just hired to help out at the family farm. Is Nicki playing hard to get, or is she hiding something? Jack knows one thing...he isn't going to rest until he finds out!

Jimmy: Jimmy Gordon has learned during his career in the Special Forces that he can handle pretty much anything, including pretending to be everything from a banquet waiter to a terrorist, while undercover. But there is one thing he finds he's having a bit of difficulty handling, and that's the governor's hot red-headed daughter, Amelia Monroe-

Carrington. Maybe the time for pretending is over?

Trilogy No. 105: Smalltown, U.S.A.

You loved Pigeon Hollow in ***Trilogy No. 103: Red Hot & Blue.*** *Now, really get to know the men of this quintessential Smalltown, U.S.A.*

The Horseman: Jared Gordon considers himself a lucky man. He enjoys the simple things life has to offer: a slice of his mama's pie, a pretty girl, a well-bred horse. Life on his farm in Pigeon Hollow is good, until big city girl Mandy Morris blows into town. Like a tornado hitting a trailer park, Mandy turns Jared's simple life upside down. Will he ever be the same again?

The Ballplayer: Cole Ryan found a life of fame and fortune in the major leagues. When an injury takes him out of the game he returns to Pigeon Hollow, the small town he thought he'd left behind. Yet every cloud has a silver lining, and for Cole that would be returning to the arms of Lizzie Barton, the small-town girl who got away a decade ago and still haunts his dreams. Will the secret she's been hiding from him all these years get in the way of their future?

The Deputy: Deputy Sheriff Bobby Barton agreed to put up with the taping of a reality TV show in his town for two reasons. He thought it would be good for the town's business, and the producers promised they'd keep out of his. But the show keeps creeping into his personal life, and he finds himself hoping that the show's assistant producer, Christy Dunne, would creep into his bed. Did Deputy Barton make a mistake that will cost him his heart?

Trilogy No. 106: Nice & Naughty

The hot firemen you loved in Opposites Attract are back with their friends, but now they're wearing a lot less clothing!

Secret Recipe: A famous lifestyle maven who secretly can't cook? Good thing a sizzling fireman who knows his way around the kitchen is there to rescue her and her holiday charity event from certain disaster. And if they detour to the bedroom on the way to the kitchen, even better!

Mr. December: What's hotter than a fireman? Twelve of them, nearly naked on the pages of your calendar! But when a rich department store owner steps in for Mr. December and meets the pretty lady photographer, things really start to heat up. He's no fireman, but that's all right. He doesn't want to put out the flames between them anyway.

Can't Buy Me Love: What do you get when you take one over-worked caterer on the brink of a nervous breakdown and add a hunky fireman for sale at the charity bachelor auction she's catering? You get a woman who finally finds the one holiday gift to buy herself that she's never going to want to return!

Trilogy No. 107: True Blue

In the long anticipated sequel to Red Hot & Blue, the true blue men of Task Force Zeta are back...and they're hotter than ever!

Bull: Bull didn't earn his nickname because he has a reputation for being stubborn; he's just a very big boy. But beneath that hard as granite and big as a mountain exterior beats the heart of a caring man. Can a pretty little thing barely five feet tall capture it?

Matt: Technical genius and communications specialist Matt Coleman is sick and tired of watching his friends 'get the girl' while the only thing he's had his hands on lately is a computer console. But perhaps Matt has been looking for love in all the wrong places. Could it be that what he's looking for has been right in front of him the entire time?

The Commander: The men in his unit refer to him as simply 'the commander'. Hank Miller may have fears, feelings, and desires, but as a leader he refuses to let them show. On more than one occasion Hank has been accused of possessing a heart of stone. When he meets the sexy and smart Lois Gordon, will the normally stoic Hank find himself tempted to break his one rule?

Trilogy No. 108: Just Desserts

Revenge may be a dish best served cold, but these three tales are hot, hot, hot!

Private Investigations: Donna is the kind of person who never thinks twice when it comes to helping a friend in need. So when her co-worker suspects her boyfriend of cheating, Donna is right there in the stakeout car next to her. Little does she know that their little foray in private investigation will lead to her own investigating of a sexy PI's privates.

Between Love and Hate: Jade thought she'd found the one, until she finds proof her boyfriend has been secretly meeting someone else. What's a girl to do? Get back at him, of course. However, sometimes things aren't always as they seem.

Saving Grace: As Valentine's Day approaches, Grace realizes all of her friends have found the loves of their lives while she is still alone and lonely. But when a secret admirer sweeps her off her feet, she discovers that Mr. Right may really be oh-so-wrong. With help from an unexpected ally, can she get free of him before she finds herself all 'tied up'?

In Heroes Unwrapped

Cuddle up by the fire with ***Heroes Unwrapped*** *- A charity anthology brought to you by the Linden Bay Romance authors. All proceeds are being donated to SOS America, Inc. in support of injured veterans.*

Under the Covers by Cat Johnson: Billy Bob "BB" Dalton thought he left his career as an underwear model behind when he became a Task Force Zeta special operative. Now they want him to be the military's new poster boy. Will the older woman assigned to manage the campaign take BB from working undercover to under the covers?

A Few Good Men

Erotic Romance author Maureen Mullen, aka Summer Winters, is on a quest. She's in pursuit of the last decent man left on earth. Week after week one loser after another has passed through Maureen's ever-revolving dating door. Now it seems opportunity is knocking in the form of deployed Army Staff Sergeant John Blake.

John gets through his days fueled by caffeine and adrenaline. A fighter, not a lover, he relies on years of training and sheer force of will. The last thing he's looking for when he accidentally becomes Maureen's pen pal is an emotional entanglement.

But when emails between the unlikely pair heat up enough to keep them both warm and wanting at night, they have to wonder if their relationship just might have potential after all. Can a hot war-hardened soldier find love in cyberspace with a sweet, hearts and flowers writer of passionate prose?

Model Soldier

Meet the one, the model soldier, Army Staff Sergeant David "Hawk" Hawkins.

Marketing executive Emily Price is accustomed to dealing with glamorous models, men and woman who are polished to perfection. When she's offered an assignment featuring one of Uncle Sam's finest soldiers, she jumps at the challenge. Who better to turn a war-hardened alpha male into a too-good-to-be-true poster boy?

Staff Sergeant David "Hawk" Hawkins is a model soldier on active duty in the Middle East. Dedicated and disciplined, he'd never imagined wanting to refuse a command or decline an assignment. Until he was ordered to work with Emily Price in the middle of a war zone on the new Army recruitment campaign featuring…him.

Packed with sexual tension, passionate love scenes, heart-stopping action, and an appearance by the men of Task Force Zeta, this long-awaited sequel to Cat Johnson's award-winning A Few Good Men will take you on a memorable, fast-paced journey that is sure to leave you wanting more.

Recommended Read:

Something About Maggie By Rose Middleton

When the love you've been searching for has been there all along...

Determined and driven, scientist Maggie Walker is used to getting what she wants—except when it comes to love. Ever since her best friend, Jack, gave her that first embarrassingly disastrous kiss at age fifteen she's yearned for a second chance to show him that they could be so much more.

Now Jack is a jet-setting freelance photographer with an enviable lifestyle. For years he's been travelling around the world to exotic locations, but when he comes home to Melbourne Maggie's always been able to count on him to be the same dependable, predictable Jack...but not this time.

From the moment Jack's plane lands he begins to see Maggie, the one person in his life he's always been sure of, in a different light. Could it just be that for the first time in a long time both Jack and Maggie are single? Possibly, although it seems to be more than that. Something unexpected has happened, something that's awakened long ignored desires and hidden passions, something that can't be ignored. This time there's no denying it, there's *Something About Maggie…*

This is a publication of

Linden Bay Romance

WWW.LINDENBAYROMANCE.COM

1918572

Made in the USA